Copyright © 2023 E.L.Boyer

Any references to historical events and with the exception of one, the names of characters are used fictitiously. Some references are made to local landmarks including restaurants and stores. Only locals will know and understand the difference.

First printing, 2023

www.boyersbookshelf.com
liz@elboyer.com

Sogale Books, LLC.

But nothing m   es a room feel
emptier than wanting
someone in it.

- Celia Quinn

This book is dedicated to all of the
missing, lost people and to the families
and friends that are looking for them
and miss them.

Proverbs 21:21
"Whoever pursues righteousness and kindness will find life, righteousness, and honor."

A
Measure
of
Kindness

———————◆———————

E. L. Boyer

Contents

Part 3

Part 4

Part 5

Prologue

◆

November 1991

Katie noticed a white van circling the block at the stop where she would normally exit the bus. The bus had to detour due to a water main break, but she could see the van going around the building she was heading for - the shelter where she volunteers. She purposely stayed on the bus and let it pass her usual stop so she could get off at the next one and keep an eye on the van. When she got off, she decided to go to the corner coffee shop before heading to the shelter. She hoped this would make it safer for her to enter the shelter without anyone following her.

A month ago, she had been part of a scheme to help a family get out of harm's way by relocating them. The shelter employees and volunteers had been told to be extra vigilant for a while, "just in case." The director was taking precautions, especially with Katie, since she was a volunteer nursing student and very young, but didn't think there would be any issue because Katie had not been seen outside the building at any time with the family.

They had all been on pins and needles because they knew Max would be back from his long-distance trucking run by now. Max did not know Katie. His only link to the shelter would be if Caroline really had seen her father's friend and if he'd recognized her and told Max. Everyone who was protecting the family thought this was a possibility, so that's how they decided to treat it. The little girl had only been outside for a second, and when she thought she'd seen her dad's friend, she ran around to the front and banged on the door. It was locked, of course, but every building has its exit points, as Caroline discovered.

Katie ordered her usual - a small coffee with heavy cream and sugar. This was no time to watch her waistline. She had been eating like a bird lately and noticed that her clothes were practically falling off her skinny frame. She had been so worried about this family and what could happen to them that she'd lost her appetite. She was also having a difficult time concentrating in her classes and hoped she could get her act together now that she believed they were safe. She finished her coffee and decided to buy a cinnamon roll for later.

She left the coffee shop, turning east toward the light. Just then the white van turned the corner and stopped right beside her.

Part - 1

Chapter - 1
Ally

Approximately thirty years later
Ally was in the process of unpacking boxes; the movers had arrived yesterday afternoon, but she had arrived a week ago, with only her clothes and a few groceries. She knew there would be kitchen utensils available, as well as bed linens and towels at her grandparent's beach house in North Carolina.

She'd given up her leased apartment in SoHo, and now the beach house had become her refuge. She had sold most of her furniture, but it had been hard to find people to buy it. Since the pandemic and resulting lockdown, people were leery of purchasing used furniture, so she had to donate some of it to various charities. She had kept some pieces that were special to her, like her hutch and table and chairs, and her chaise lounge. She wasn't sure where they would fit in the beach house but she still wanted to have them there. Then there was the artwork she had collected over the years that she could not part with yet. She would store most of it in one of the spare bedrooms until she decided if she would keep it.

The pandemic had upset her life, as it had the rest of the world. After being a nurse for thirty years, she'd been let go because she, along with a few of her co-workers, had refused to take the vaccine. She thought about all those countless hours of hard work during the pandemic, and of the love and praise lavished on her and her colleagues by fellow New Yorkers. But when they'd decided not to take the vaccine, the administration had stood by the CDC and informed them they would have to be let go. She knew it had been a hard decision for them because they were in unchartered territory. The vaccine had become available at lightning speed, under orders from the federal government, and the usual protocols of testing had not been conducted. The administration had even labeled it "Warp Speed," so Ally had made the difficult decision to put her personal concerns ahead of her employer's demands. She would have to live with that decision. She hated leaving so many friends but hoped they would stay in touch. Only time would tell.

It was not that she was against vaccines. After all, she got the flu shot every year. She just believed that after being exposed so often to the Covid-19 virus, she didn't need exposure to a vaccine she knew nothing about. She had begun to lose confidence in her government and even in her hospital administrators. To make matters worse, in addition to losing her job and vocation, she had ended a two-year relationship with her boyfriend.

He was a lab technician she'd met at a co-worker's wedding in 2019. They'd hit it off even though they didn't have much in common. He was two years her junior, divorced and from Brooklyn. He was very handsome and she did enjoy his company when they had a chance to be together. He worked at a private laboratory and lived in lower Manhattan. There was no doubt that his roots were in the city. He had a big Italian family and two children, a twelve-year-old boy named Gabe, his namesake, and a darling little girl of nine named Sophia. She knew he would never consider moving away from the city. Besides, they had argued over her decision to refuse the vaccine. He'd shouted at her, "You're giving up your entire career over a stupid vaccine!" Nevertheless, they parted as amicably as possible. She told him to call her when he visits Myrtle Beach, where she knew his family liked to vacation. She knew she would miss his children even more than she would miss him. She'd never wanted children herself but had grown fond of his.

Now, here she was at fifty-two, without a job and having to depend on her family. Fortunately, her grandmother had kept the beach house they had gone to for so many summers as children. It was a great house and was built up on stilts, as most are to protect them against storm surges from hurricanes. It was rustic looking, nothing fancy, and you had to walk up a very long flight of stairs to reach it. Luckily, there was a landing halfway up. The front deck faced the ocean but it currently lacked deck furniture, so sitting out there to enjoy the view was not possible. The décor inside was circa 1970's, so pretty retro, but for now she had everything she needed.

Her mother had inherited the beach house when her grandmother had died of the Covid-19 virus. Grandma Harriett was the quintessential grandmother. she adored and doted on her three grandchildren, Ally and her two siblings. She'd lived alone in an assisted living place near Ally's mother in Florida. She had been doing well after having hip replacement surgery but then the pandemic hit. She had just returned to her living arrangements when one night she had trouble breathing and had to be rushed to the emergency room. Ally's mother had hurried to the hospital and stayed with her, but Grandma Harriett passed away the next day. It happened so fast, and since the world was on lockdown, no one in the family except Ally's mother was able to see her before she died. Her funeral was six months later in New York. She'd been cremated, and her ashes were buried next to Ally's grandfather's grave. May she rest in peace, thought Ally sadly. They had all loved her very much.

Ally's sister and brother hadn't wanted to bother with the beach house and her parents lived in Florida now, and had no interest in maintaining it or renting it out. They lived too far away to become landlords, with all the hassle that entailed, and wanted to live a simpler life. They could have sold it, of course, but since she was suddenly jobless and about to become homeless, they took pity on her and told her to take it with their blessings. It would need some work, but she was up to the challenge and would take her time to make it more comfortable. She knew her casual style would fit in well with the beach vibe. Though the house wasn't on the water, it was only about a ten-minute walk to the public access beach, so that's where Ally decided to go now.

The street on which the house sat was a dead end and very quiet. As she walked along, she noticed the tide appeared to be out and she could just make out a shrimp boat in the distance. She didn't know much about beach life but was determined to learn quickly, since she intended to be here for a while. She walked along the edge of the water, but jumped back to keep her shoes from getting wet. She'd started walking here every day since she'd moved in and looking for seashells had become a habit. She picked up a few that were not broken and decided to start a collection. She'd found a small book about shells in a drawer at the house, so she would use that as a reference to study them and find out more about the ones she collected.

After a while, she returned to the house and washed off her feet and legs at the outdoor shower. She went in and threw on her gray sweats and her NC State T-shirt. She didn't follow any particular college sports team, but when she saw the T-shirt at the local Walgreen's, she figured it would be a good way to blend in with the locals. For now, she still followed the Yankees and Jets, and kept up with her alma mater, Syracuse University, especially the basketball team.

In her short time in North Carolina so far, she'd found the locals to be quite nice. The ironic thing was that many of them were not actually native North Carolinians. Almost everyone she had met was from the northeast: New Jersey, New York, Massachusetts and Pennsylvania. They all had a similar story - tired of the taxes and the snow. Ally herself had not yet taken the time to look into the property taxes here in North Carolina, especially since the deed was still in her mother's name, but since she was now living there, she knew her mother would rather she take care of the taxes and maintenance. Her mother had always been a stickler about her children being independent. Ally hoped she would eventually turn over the deed to her since she would be the one living there, paying the property taxes, and making any improvements to it. She didn't expect any squabbles with her siblings over ownership of the house either, since they all got along pretty well, and since they were mostly settled in their own lives, it was unlikely they would even care about the house.

She snuggled on the tattered sofa in the living room with her newly found tabby cat. It had shown up on her front porch two nights earlier and looked so sweet that she had to bring it in. A neighbor had warned her that once in a while she might see a feral cat roaming around, but since they helped keep the rodent population down, the neighbors didn't mind the odd stray or two. Ally believed that the kitten on her porch might have been dropped off by someone, since there didn't appear to be any other littermates around and it looked very young. She had never had a cat or dog because of her hectic and unpredictable work schedule and the places she'd lived had always prohibited pets, but she had always wanted a fur baby, so she was excited to finally have one. She made a mental note to find a veterinarian and take the kitten in for a check-up. She'd already run out for kitten food, a cat bowl, litter and a litter box. She'd added a small stuffed gray mouse that squeaked when squeezed, but the kitten had so far ignored it. She was relieved that it at least seemed to know what to do with the litter box. She had no idea if she was allergic to cats but so far, she had not sneezed or broken out in a rash or anything, so she was hoping for the best

She hadn't really met anyone she could ask to join her for dinner, and was uncomfortable going alone but didn't have what she needed to cook something, so she found the local Zaxby's and bought what looked like a healthful salad. Her father's words came back to her as she thought about the distinction between healthy and healthful: 'Ally, people are healthy but things that can make you healthy are health*ful*.' Now every time she hears someone on TV talk about something that's healthy for you, she recalls her father's words. Sometimes she even yells at the screen to correct the speaker. She considered all the advice her father had given her in life and took a moment to reflect. *Thanks, Dad, for keeping me straight,* she thought.

Since she was eating alone, she decided to get the television working. It was an old one and she didn't yet have cable or internet, but she had found rabbit ears in the hall closet and hooked them up. She found a local channel and saw that the news has just started. The lead story was about pieces of a skeleton that had been found on the local beach, the one she'd been walking along every day since she'd moved there. Apparently, the Turtle Patrol had discovered the skeleton a couple of weeks ago but the media had just been informed that the remains had been identified. Ally's jaw dropped open when she heard the name…it was a name from her own past.

Chapter - 2

Ally thought she'd heard it wrong, but as she listened more closely, she heard the newscaster repeat the name Kathryn Morgan. The reporter explained that the body apparently had been covered in a tarp and tied with cord. The authorities, he said, speculated it must have been weighed down with something because it seemed to have been in the water for a very long time. Yes, Ally knew that if it was the Kathryn Morgan she knew, then it was a very long time, in fact, since 1991. She'd zoned out for a minute, but then heard the reporter say the skull was among the remains and was miraculously still attached to the torso, so dental forensics was able to make a positive identification. How they were able to obtain the dental records so quickly was not explained but Ally assumed they were in a database somewhere.

What a shock it must be to Katie's family. All that time wondering what had happened to their daughter. She had no idea if Katie's parents were still alive, or if she would be able to locate them even if they were. Without her computer, she couldn't get more information, so she would just have to wait. She used her phone to see if there was any further information out there, but everyone had the same story.

Ally thought about the day Katie had disappeared. It was in 1991, during the fall semester of her senior year of nursing school at Syracuse University and she'd disappeared under unusual circumstances. The details were fuzzy all these years later, but Ally recalled that Katie had been clandestinely seeing an older man. Her roommates had no idea who the 'mystery man' was but they were curious as to why Katie would not talk about him. The closest they came to knowing any more was when one of them happened to be at their dorm window one day and saw Katie get into a black Jaguar. They assumed it was the 'mystery man'. After she went missing, the police followed up on the lead but never came up with the identity of the man. Katie's parents had called her dormitory floor phone the Friday before she was reported missing and when no one could track her down after they'd called several times, her parents contacted campus police. Apparently she'd been in her class on Thursday morning but her class on Friday had been cancelled, so no one could determine her whereabouts that day. He three roommates had been off campus since Friday afternoon but didn't remember seeing her Friday morning, and figured she had either left for home the day before or stayed with a friend on campus. All three girls had solid alibis, so the police quickly cleared them of any involvement.

The police had questioned everyone in the dormitory as to their whereabouts for the previous two days. All Ally could remember was being in some classes with Katie, but they weren't really friends or anything. It was about two weeks before Thanksgiving break, after which they would have finals. At the time, Ally was dating a pre-med student, Hank Bowyer, who'd told her that everyone in his dorm had also been questioned. She remembered how helpless everyone felt. A college campus was considered a 'safe' place, but suddenly it didn't feel so safe anymore.

Initially, the police thought she might've left of her own accord, but then they found too many troubling things they couldn't explain and determined that she must've been a victim of foul play. For instance, her roommates realized she had not been in the room for about forty-eight hours, because her clothes had not been touched and one of the girls had borrowed a sweater and laid it on her bed, but it was still laying there two days later. She told the police, "Katie was a bit of a neat freak and she would've put it away as soon as she'd seen it."

Rumors swarmed all over campus, fueled by what her roommates told the police, about whether she could've been seeing someone off campus and had simply decided to leave and start a new life. Ally never thought that was possible because she knew Katie was very studious and seemed committed to becoming a nurse. Her absence was felt by everyone. In such tight quarters, the absence of one person is noticed. Ally remembered seeing a girl in the bathroom one night just sobbing. Her name was Beth. She remembered it because she loved Little Women and the girl reminded her of the Beth portrayed in the movie. Ally had asked her what was wrong and she said she couldn't stop thinking about Katie. They'd been in Anatomy II together and she missed seeing her. She was convinced that she'd been kidnapped and she would never see her again. Ally tried to comfort her but they both just started sobbing.

A pall fell over the whole campus. The school was still grieving the loss of thirty-five students in the plane crash over Lockerbie, Scotland in December of 1988, just three years earlier. They'd been returning from a trip when a bomb exploded, killing 259 passengers and crew and another 11 people on the ground. No one had ever been brought to justice and it was still being investigated when Katie went missing. Ally's boyfriend had known one of the students because he lived in his dormitory. It happened during Ally's first year of college and she'd never forgotten it.

When Ally went home for Thanksgiving that year, she told her family about Katie. They were very upset, of course, but thought she would probably show up. "Maybe she just needed some time to be by herself," her mother had suggested. "She may be considering another career." Ally knew that wasn't the case but let her mother believe it anyway. She was glad she was able to see her grandparents that year and realized how precious family was to her. You just never knew when you might not see them again.

When she returned to school, there was still no sign of Katie and the police seemed to be at a loss for clues. The nursing dormitory held a campus vigil in Katie's honor. Her parents and brothers were there for it. No one could imagine what her family was going through. Signs had been put up all over town by then. Ally had heard that some students who hadn't gone home for Thanksgiving had helped put up the flyers. But eventually, life returned to normal. Classes resumed and it was full steam ahead toward finals, followed by Christmas break. Katie's parents cleared out her dorm room after the police searched and dusted it for forensic evidence, but in the end they had no suspect. The news media had been running the story daily, but that too started to wane over time.

Now, thirty years later, her skeleton had washed up. *What on earth?* thought Ally. *How can a skeleton wash up after all these years?* she wondered. She knew she needed her computer so she could follow the case online.

Chapter - 3

The following morning, Ally awoke to a beautiful clear blue sky. She felt like she was in paradise. It was April, over two years since the pandemic had reared its ugly head and six months since she'd lost her job. She was very glad now that she had saved as much money as she had over the years. She was glad she'd gotten that gene from her mother's side of the family. After the 2008 economic collapse, when her 403b had taken a big hit, she decided to decrease her contribution by a small percentage and started religiously putting the difference into a Roth IRA. She wanted to have more liquid assets that she would be able to access when necessary. Sure, it meant she would lose on the front end, with more tax being taken out of her paycheck, but as a single woman she needed to protect herself.

She even started buying silver and gold. She consulted her father about it first and he went to his financial planner, who told him which one she should look into. "You have to be careful when it comes to knowing who to trust," her father had warned her, but he didn't need to worry; she was already suspicious of people when it came to finances. After 9/11 and the aftermath in the financial world, followed by the 2008 economic meltdown, Ally worried more about the future. She had actually considered investing in a friend's small restaurant in New York's SoHo district in order to diversify her portfolio, hoping it would be successful and she would eventually make money on it. But now she was glad she'd rejected the idea, because the pandemic had decimated the restaurant industry. Her friend was still not sure if his restaurant was going to survive. Even with the Paycheck Protection money from the government, he still had significant debts and concerns.

When she was laid off, Ally had to decide whether to try to make it in New York in another field, but in the end she knew she was only qualified to be a nurse. Since she had a safety net and a place to go, she decided to leave New York, a city she loved. Besides, the restrictions in the city were so extreme, life had become very unpleasant. Her mother was the one who mentioned the beach house, reminding Ally that it had been vacant for a long time. The family had stopped using it as a vacation spot by the time the children were teenagers. Her grandparents had stopped going because it was too long a trip for them and they never wanted to live there permanently. After mulling it over and with no other viable options, she decided to take her mother up on her offer. She knew moving to a new town alone would be scary, but she also didn't want to go as far as Florida because she hates hot weather and because her parents and brother, Craig, were already there. Four's a crowd, she thought. Her sister Janet had moved to Texas after she'd married several years earlier, and she and her husband Adam had two children, who were now teenagers. Ally knew Janet has her hands full, with no time for much else. In fact, her nephew was in college. *How had that happened?* Ally wondered. *I must be getting old, she mused.*

The beach house needed work but she'd have plenty of time for that now. The first thing she wanted to do was replace the sofa. But she also realized it would be nice to find a job, so it was time to get moving.

She called an internet service provider to set up an appointment for tomorrow morning, then showered, fed the kitten and set off for Publix to get a newspaper. She returned home to troll the want ads in the paper in the privacy of her house as she ate her breakfast of Muesli with fresh strawberries and drank strong coffee. She knew she was in a tourist town and the majority of jobs were service jobs, like waitressing and housekeeping. She also saw several hospitals with ads looking for nurses and offering huge bonuses. It was tempting, but after six months away, she didn't feel ready to try again. She kept her RN license active and intended to do so as long as she could but she doubted she would ever go back. She hated that she'd had to leave her life's vocation that she loved and had worked so hard at, and continued to harbor resentment about the way it was handled.

She noticed several waitressing jobs, but that did not sound at all appealing. Just when she was about to give up, she noticed an ad for a catering assistant. She called the number provided and a deep-voiced male answered. She explained she was calling about the catering position but before she could ask any questions, he asked if she could come in for an interview at three o'clock today. She got the feeling he was pressed for time so she said, "Sure."

She wondered if it was that easy of a job that they would hire just any warm body. She hoped not. A catering job, she thought, requires honest people, who are punctual and reliable. She knew she would pass any background check, of course, since she had never had so much as a speeding ticket, especially since she'd done very little driving in her lifetime. She'd finally gotten her license when she turned nineteen, but that was only because her mother wanted her to have transportation home from college so she wouldn't have to drop everything and pick her up every time. Her parents had bought her a used Honda Accord and she kept that car in a garage in New York for years after she graduated and went to work in the city. She finally figured out that paying the garage fees weren't worth it and sold it to a coworker's son for a pittance. When she needed to go home, she would simply rent a vehicle. She walked everywhere possible in the city and took the subway for longer distances. She missed the city, or rather the city as it used to be. She didn't think she could ever live there again.

Since she had some time before she had to leave for the interview, she decided to set up a place for her laptop. She managed to move an old desk out of a spare bedroom and into the living room. It was more crowded, certainly, but she preferred to have her office space near the front of the house. She then went closet diving and found a pair of gray slacks and a Talbot's freshly laundered shirt. She just needed to locate her iron and ironing board to give it a crisp look. She was satisfied when she examined herself in the mirror that she looked like a professional caterer, whatever that meant.

Chapter - 4

On her way to her interview in Southport, she stopped at a Walmart to purchase a Roku for the TV so she would be ready when the internet was installed. Her timing was perfect. She had no trouble finding Three Island Catering. It was a small building that looked more like a home that had been converted into a business. She parked out front and walked to the front door, spying a small trailer out back. She guessed it was a portable catering vehicle. There was also a medium-sized truck that looked like it could hold enough food for a small army. Inside she was greeted by Sara, the receptionist, whose name was printed on a placard on the desk. Sara was a tall, bottle blonde with a picture of Elvis on her desk, circa mid 1960's. She handed Ally a clear yellow clipboard with a one-page application to be filled out. Ally helped herself to one of the yellow pens in a cup with Elvis pictures on them that sat on the desk.

The application was straightforward: name, address, social security number. Ally sat in one of two well-worn chairs with a lamp between them. The room décor was casual and had additional dim lighting in the ceiling tiles.

At three-fifteen, the front door opened and in stepped a strikingly handsome man with sandy gray hair and piercing green eyes, dressed in khakis and a light blue polo shirt with a *Three Island Catering* logo in the upper left corner. He introduced himself as Eugene Talbott but told Ally to call him Gene. He led her down the hall to his office, which was exceptionally neat and organized. Ally waited for him to begin the interview, which he did with a simple question. "Have you ever waitressed or catered before?" he asked without preamble.

Since they hadn't requested any employment history or references on the application, he obviously had no idea how she would respond. She almost quipped, "I delivered food to patients for thirty years, so I think I qualify," but luckily, she thought better of allowing her residual bitterness to show itself in a sarcastic remark and instead put on her professional face to answer honestly, "No."

"Well, that shouldn't be a problem. What did you do before?" he asked.

Ally told him she was an RN.

"Really?" asked Gene, with unexpected curiosity. "Any desire to continue with that? I know hospitals are looking for nurses because so many have quit."

Ally confessed that she had chosen not to be vaccinated but did not go into her reasons and Gene didn't ask. Then it occurred to her that it might be a problem in this type of job, so she asked him if it would be an issue.

"No, I trust my caterers to let me know if they feel sick. If they need to get tested, I help them find a place to do that. Most of my caterers are young and healthy. Not that they couldn't be carriers, I guess, but it hasn't come up with my customers since things have started getting back to normal. I think we can take a chance on you," he said, and he winked at her.

They discussed the job requirements, and he told her his business was bonded and insured so that covered anyone who works for him. He said he trusts his employees, that they are loyal and all watch each other's backs. Availability is on an as-needed and as-available basis. He said he couldn't guarantee hours so he doesn't ask his employees to guarantee that they're always available. He explained he has a crew that takes care of delivery and clean up, so she wouldn't be expected to do any heavy lifting. He assured her that no one had ever complained nor had he had any disability claims against him. Finally, he shared a bit of his personal life and background, which made Ally feel much more at ease. He said he was a native North Carolinian from the Outer Banks, and that he'd grown up in several towns along the coast. He was the only child of a single mother, who'd taught him all he knew about cooking and preparing. He'd worked for the business since high school, and when the owner passed away, he managed to purchase it and moved it to where it was now. "I never looked back; this area is the best of the best when it comes to beaches in North Carolina."

He asked if she thought she could do the job and if she was interested. To both questions she answered, "Yes, absolutely."

He assured her he would be in touch in a couple of days to let her know if she was hired. "I have two more interviews to complete and I have only one opening right now," he explained.

On her drive home, Ally found an upscale consignment shop and, with the help of the owner, she purchased a small sofa and matching chair. They were cream-colored and in very good condition. She arranged to have it delivered in two days and the owner said for a fee she would also remove the old furniture and bring it to the local dump. Ally thanked her and promised to be back when she decided how she wanted to decorate her new place. All the way home, she had Gene with the striking good looks on her mind.

But when she pulled into her driveway and stepped out of the car, she heard a voice behind her. She turned and saw a woman approaching with what she assumed was a casserole.

"Hi there. I'm Mary Hughes. Welcome to the neighborhood," greeted the woman, handing Ally the dish. She said she lived across the street, two house down, and just wanted to say hello.

Ally thanked her and accepted the dish, which appeared to be baked ziti, then invited her to come inside. Mary said she didn't want to impose but accepted the invitation.

Ally apologized for the dated and bare furnishings. "I'm slowly trying to improve the place." She explained that the house had been left to her mother by her grandmother and had not been used for several years. "I just purchased a sofa and chair today, as a matter of fact, so the tattered one over there will be removed in a couple of days. She pointed at the kitten lying on the sofa and added with a smile, "Obviously, my new little housemate will be staying. She showed up on the front porch a few nights ago and is making herself at home, but I don't mind at all!" She smiled at the kitten, who was now making its way over to investigate the visitor. Ally realized she'd have to name her pretty soon, assuming it was a her, though Ally had no idea how to determine its gender. Another reason they had to get to the vet soon.

"I brought down a hutch and table and chairs, and a chaise from New York, and they're stored in the extra bedroom," she continued. "I haven't decided if I'll keep them but if I do I'll get rid of my grandmother's set. Maybe you'll come back and help me decide," she suggested, hoping she'd found a new friend.

"Absolutely!" said Mary enthusiastically. "Decorating is my hobby; I even went to school for interior design and worked in Connecticut for a while." She told Ally she'd married a wonderful man, moved to Philadelphia and raised four sons. "Tom and the boys were my life. Unfortunately, I lost Tom to cancer five years ago." She began to get choked up but then went on. "The boys are grown and well on their way and don't need their mother anymore. I finally decided a change of location would be good for me and I've always liked the beach, so I sold everything and bought my house here. It's large enough for my grandkids to visit, since I won't always be able to go to them."

Ally could tell that Mary probably needed a friend as much as she did and was delighted to meet her. "Maybe you'd like to stay for dinner? You brought it, after all." They both laughed and Mary said she'd love to. "And how about we have a glass of wine now?" offered Ally.

By the time they'd finished the first glass of wine, Ally felt like they'd bonded. Mary was about the same age as her and looked to be in great shape. "How do you stay so fit?" Ally asked enviously over their second glass.

"I joined the fitness center at the local community college. It's a great place and they have a pool. It's not just for the college kids; it was built for the entire county by a woman named Dinah Gore, so they named it after her – the Dinah E. Gore Fitness and Aquatics Center. It's very reasonably priced, too." Mary seemed to think Ally might want to know that, probably after assessing her minimalist furnishings.

Ally thanked her and said she'd look into it very soon, then asked if maybe they could go together. "I walk along the beach every day but I'm sure I need some cardio and some toning, if you know what I mean." They both laughed.

Ally warmed up the baked ziti, made a small salad and opened her favorite red wine. They laughed and enjoyed their evening, learning more about each other and exchanging stories of snow up north and how they'd each found this particular paradise. Mary left before it got too dark, but they agreed to go consignment store shopping together in the next week or so. "I don't want to go gangbusters on decorating but I know I need to update the place a bit. I'm just gonna have to be careful with my money until I'm gainfully employed again."

"Hey, since you're a nurse, why not apply at the local hospitals?" Mary asked, hoping Ally didn't think the question was too personal so early in their friendship.

Ally told her the truth, that she had refused to take the vaccine and it ultimately led to her losing her job. "Now I'm so burned out with nursing that I don't want to go back to it. It was a great career choice but I'm ready to explore other things."

Mary warned her that there were limited jobs in the region because it was not exactly a metropolis.

Ally said, "Yeah, I've figured that out from looking at want ads. And I'm afraid if I get on LinkedIn right now all I'll get are tons of emails about nursing jobs. Of course that's not even an issue right now because my computer isn't even hooked up yet. But you know what? I actually had an interview today to work for a caterer and it sounds exciting. You know, something different. And then I met you! So I feel like all of this is a great way to begin a new life. There's no telling what's in store, right?" she said happily.

Mary smiled broadly and agreed as they said good night.

Chapter - 5

As she was cleaning up after Mary left, Ally began thinking about her life choices. She had never married nor ever even been close to marrying. She thought she was attractive, and had been told so many times over the years. At five-foot-six, a hundred and twenty pounds, and with long, light brown hair and hazel eyes, in her youth she had been considered as a potential contestant in a beauty pageant in her hometown, but to her mother's dismay, she chose not to enter. She was a runner so had always been fit. She'd never had a problem getting dates and had a few steady boyfriends in college, but never really fell in love or wanted to marry. Her sister, Janet, on the other hand, had always yearned to be married. She had known her husband, Adam, since grade school and it seemed they were destined to marry. They'd both attended Syracuse University and after graduating, Adam had gone on to Columbia Law School. He was now a defense attorney at a huge law firm in Waco, Texas, handling mostly business clients.

Janet had majored in early elementary education, but never used her degree because they married right after graduation. Instead, she worked in the city while Adam attended Columbia, and when he received the job offer in Texas, they decided to be adventurous and move there. Neither of them had ever lived anywhere but New York, but they had each other and a good job offer, so it turned out to be the right decision. Ally's mother hated to see her daughter move so far away but knew Janet was in good hands with Adam. He was a great husband and able to be a good provider, and she wanted Janet to be happy.

Unfortunately, Janet had difficulty getting pregnant and they went through a myriad of tests. She miscarried twice, but just as they were about to consider adoption proceedings, she became pregnant with Justin in 2000. Janet was thirty-two at the time. It had been a difficult pregnancy, made worse by a difficult delivery, but she came through it and two years gave birth to their second child, Rachel.

Since Janet's life was settled and seemed to be going according to plan, Ally's mother often probed her about her social life, wondering if she had a boyfriend, if it was serious, and all the usual motherly questions. Ally did her best to keep her answers vague and protect her privacy. She never brought anyone home to meet her family. And once she graduated and moved to the city, she had little chance or time to date anyway. When she did, she found men were only interesting up to a point. She would avoid meeting their family, knowing that was the sign they were interested in taking the relationship further and she was not ready for that. At some point, she realized that she loved the chase but not the catch. She liked dating Wall Street bankers because they had money to take her to shows and nice restaurants. But they also expected a little something extra, and sometimes she would comply but others she would drop like a hot potato. She avoided dating medical residents because unless they were trust fund babies, they didn't have money, and besides, it would be awkward if they worked together.

Her mother would ask her if she'd found a doctor to marry, but Ally's answer was always the same. "No, mother, they're all already married." Her mother would squint at her suspiciously, as if to say, 'You've been telling me that for ten years now'. Eventually, her mother gave up and was satisfied that at least Janet had given her two grandchildren.

Ally's family was what might be considered middle class, but she knew that was not entirely true. Her mother came from old money and had had a trust fund since she was twenty-five, left to her by her paternal grandfather. He was a billionaire before that term was in the national conversation. Great grandfather Elias, as they called him, was a genius and a real estate magnate. He'd started his empire purchasing small dwellings around New York City, mainly in the Bronx. By the time he was thirty, he owned over a hundred rentals. He was a kind man but a stern landlord. He even wrote a book in the 50's about being a landlord. It sold rather well, Ally had been told. She figured there must be a copy of it somewhere in the beach house, and made a mental note to look around for it. It was a forerunner of the modern 'how to' books. So yes, the Stanleys, her mother's side of the family, were very rich, but were also a hardworking family and wanted their offspring to do well.

Ally's father, on the other hand, did not come from wealth but was proud of what he had become. John Malcom, who considered himself more of a scientist, owned his own pharmacy in a small town named Eldridge, just outside of Syracuse in upstate New York. Ally's parents believed Eldridge was an ideal place to raise a family. Ally was the youngest. She'd done well in school and excelled in math and science. She'd always wanted to be a nurse and her father had encouraged her. She wasn't necessarily the nurturing type but she was sensitive to people in pain and always wanted to be the one to apply the band aid to one of her siblings. Her mother didn't really care what direction Ally took in life but had always said, 'A woman can be anything she wants to be; those who have gone before you have paved the way for you to succeed." She gave Janet the same advice, but Janet only ever wanted to marry Adam and have children. Ally had always wondered why her mother, who did not work, felt so strongly about women choosing their own path, but it never occurred to her to ask her mother about her views.

When they were growing up, Malcom Pharmacy was the only pharmacy in town. By the time Ally graduated high school and was preparing to go off to college, Eldridge's population had significantly increased, and the larger chain pharmacies were moving into town. Eventually her father had sold out to Rite Aid for a handsome sum and retired to fishing and golf, though Ally and her siblings had no idea how much he'd sold it for because her parents never discussed finances with their children.

John and Gloria Malcom were social and enjoyed the local country club. In 2012, ten years after her father had sold the store, they decided to sell the snow blower and move to Florida to escape the cold, central New York weather. They moved to a town in central Florida called Bartow. It was just their kind of town - quaint and quiet. Her mother's aunt had lived there for many years. Gloria remembered visiting her as a child and told Ally's father that it had everything they needed. She even said, "The movie, *My Girl,* was filmed in one of the beautiful homes there." That did not impress him, but then she added, "If company comes to town, they probably won't stay long because it's so far from the beaches." That sold him on it and they'd never looked back. Then a few years ago, Ally's brother Craig had moved to Tampa with his live-in girlfriend to pursue his passion, sports medicine, so they were thrilled to have at least one of their children less than an hour away.

As for Ally, she had always lived frugally. As much as she loved the beautiful couture of New York City fashion, she loved her bank account more. A simple Chico's outfit suited her just fine. Now that she was unemployed, she was thankful she had always been sensible with her money. When she was laid off, she chose to take the COBRA option to continue her healthcare coverage, and had been paying the insurance premiums for six months now, but knew she would have to find her own coverage in another six months, when the year ended. She had to admit, she certainly hoped to hear from handsome Gene tomorrow, for more than one reason.

Chapter - 6

The internet service provider said they would be there that morning to install her service, so Ally rose early in case they came earlier than expected. When she'd stopped in their office to make the appointment, the girl who took her order said absently that they were extremely busy lately because of all of the northerners moving down there, then seemed a little embarrassed by having said too much. Ally just smiled and nodded knowingly, making the girl feel more at ease.

While she waited for the installers to show, she fed the cat and thought about a name for it. She didn't know whether it was a male or female, so she named it Lucky, which seemed somewhat gender-neutral. She just felt like the little kitten was lucky to have found her and she herself was lucky to have it for company. She pulled out the new phone book she'd found when she arrived at the beach house and started looking for a vet in the area. She found one nearby and called them, and they told her the wait time for new patients was two weeks, which was fine with her. It would give her time to check off other things on her to-do list.

The internet guy didn't show up until eleven fifteen, but it didn't take him long to get everything hooked up. He even got her Roku up and working. "Everyone is switching to streaming," he told her. He showed her how her internet could work both through the TV and using her laptop. He suggested she think about buying a newer TV, of course. "Everything would work better and look sharper on a newer model." *Right after the washer and dryer, the vet appointment and a few other pressing things,* she thought as she nodded. She thanked him and offered him something to drink but he declined. "I'm good, I've got plenty in the truck." She realized they probably had to think about staying well hydrated in this heat, especially when they're working outside on poles for long periods of time.

With internet service and a vet appointment scheduled, Ally was slowly but surely getting things in order. She found a nearby appliance/hardware store and bought a GE washer and dryer, the same one her grandmother had always had. She wasn't well versed on how to choose appliances so she figured it was best to stick with what her grandparents had used for so many years. She also looked at the stoves and refrigerators but decided to wait on those until she knew whether or not she had a job. But she was happy to pick up a few smaller things, like a new pair of gardening gloves for weeding and some ant spray. She recalled from childhood visits that the fire ants down here were deadly.

She returned home and for the next two hours, Ally waited for a call from Gene. Just as she was about to give up, he called. He said Sara needed her last three places of employment and at least three non-family references. She reminded him that she'd told him she'd been laid off for refusing to take the vaccine, and explained that the hospital had been the only place she had ever worked.

There was a momentary silence on the other end of the line, long enough that Ally thought the connection might've been dropped, but then he said, "I guess I'd forgotten you were a nurse. Okay, we'll go with the one job reference. If your personal references check out, you'll have the job. When can you start?"

Ally was practically speechless with happiness but managed to say, "Any time."

Gene said Sara would be calling shortly to get her references and thanked her for her time. She thanked him for the opportunity.

Ally thought with a smile, *Sara, the Elvis fan, will be calling my former employer in New York City.* She wondered if Sara had ever been to the Big Apple? She wasn't worried about what they would say. She knew that for legal reasons employers only gave out minimal information and other than her vaccine refusal, which she had already disclosed to Gene, there was nothing on her record that would be an issue anyway. Her other references would be coworkers and a neighbor where she used to live, so she was confident it would go smoothly and that the job was in the bag.

Ally had been thinking about the news story about the remains washed up on the beach and decided to google Katie Morgan to see if there were any further updates. A picture popped up as soon as she entered Katie's name into the search field. Of course, she was frozen in time as a 21-year-old college student. She was so beautiful. She had long brown hair and blue eyes. The article said she'd been identified quickly because her parents lived close by and when they heard about the remains found on the beach, they immediately contacted the Brunswick County Sheriff's Department and told them they had a missing child and had her dental records in their possession. They were nevertheless shocked by the awful news; Katie had been their only daughter. The article did not disclose where they lived but Ally very much wanted to reach out to them, so she decided to call the Sheriff's office to see if they could help her get in touch.

As soon as she mentioned the body on the beach (though it was really just a skeleton), she was put through to a female detective named Hernandez. Ally explained that she had been a classmate of Katie Morgan's, who'd disappeared in 1991. She told Detective Hernandez that she would like to contact Katie's parents, if for no other reason than to offer her condolences, but she didn't know how to find them. She didn't know if she could be of further assistance but Detective Hernandez took down her phone number and told her she would pass it along to the family, and if they wished to make contact, it would be up to them. She thanked her for the call and her concern.

Ally had never been involved in any criminal proceedings and had no idea how the system worked. Sure, she had watched *Hill Street Blues* and the occasional *Law and Order* back in the day but had not followed any of the True Crime genre that had become so popular in the last decade or so. The O. J. Simpson trial had mesmerized the nation, which now seemed in the throes of reality murder. There were countless TV shows about real life crimes but as a nurse, Ally experienced enough heartache when one of her patients died. She'd been working in the ICU during the pandemic, so the last thing she wanted to do when she got home was to see more death on TV. Comedy was her jam. She loved *Seinfeld and Will and Grace reruns.* Dated, yes, but still funny, and a great escape from reality.

He ex-boyfriend had told her that there were podcasts about everything these days. Apparently, they'd become enormously popular during the pandemic, when people were stuck at home. Out of curiosity, Ally decided to google true crime podcasts. So many popped up that she didn't know where to start, but after reading about a few of them, she found one that looked interesting. It was called Going West and she was intrigued about what "*going west*" had to do with true crime.

She got it on the Apple podcasts app. She didn't listen to music on her phone, so she'd never downloaded any platforms like Spotify and wasn't interested in learning how just yet, although she would consider it if she joined the gym. It would certainly pass the time to have a playlist ready if she was on a treadmill. The Apple podcast did not require a download. She picked the first episode that came up. It was forty-four minutes long so she made a salad while she listened. It was fascinating. The voices of the hosts were so captivating she forgot she was listening to the worst thing that could happen to anyone. When it was over, she looked through the more than 150 shows to see if they had done one on Katie, but they had not. The hosts did say that anyone could email them about a potential show and they might put it on air, but they were very backed up at the moment. *How awful it is that there are that many missing and murdered people,* thought Ally.

Chapter - 7

Another day dawned, with a brilliant clear blue sky. "I never get tired of blue skies," Ally said to Lucky. He, or she, was curled up beside her and not yet ready to stir. "Are you nocturnal? Have you been up all night?" she laughed, but her new fur baby simply stretched and re-positioned him (or her)self. She decided to go for a walk on the beach, and threw on a pair of shorts and a hoodie. When she got there, she realized the tide was coming in so she knew she wouldn't find any shells. She was beginning to understand the seasons and why the beach seemed to be busier now than it had been only a couple of weeks ago. It was spring break now which meant it would be busy for a while, then summer would be upon them before she knew it. She had not been wearing sunscreen on her walks but decided she'd better pick some up the next time she went shopping. She remembered her grandmother having some skin cancers removed and Ally had her grandmother's light skin, so she wanted to be careful.

By the time she'd returned and showered, Lucky was awake and meowing with hunger so she fed him before sitting down with her morning coffee and breakfast. She turned on the TV and saw the weather report was predicting a storm this afternoon. She decided to call the store where she'd bought her new sofa and chair when it opened at nine o'clock to find out if they would be delivered before the storm. She glanced at her phone and saw she had two voicemails that must've come in while she was in the shower. One was from the handsome Gene telling her she had the job if she still wanted it. He added that he could actually use her at a function this coming Saturday, which was only two days from now. He asked her to call him back ASAP to confirm. Yes sir! she thought as she smiled.

The other message was from Mrs. Morgan, Katie's mom. The message asked her to return the call. She said she heard through a message from Detective Hernandez that Ally wanted to talk with her. Ally was pleased to hear that the detective had done what she'd promised and relieved that her request was welcomed by Katie's mother. First she returned Gene's call and left a message on his voicemail telling him that she definitely still wanted the job and could work this Saturday. She asked him to call her with details and asked what she should wear or whether there was a uniform she would need to purchase.

She was not mentally ready to speak with Mrs. Morgan, so instead she called the consignment shop to find out what time they would deliver the furniture. Debbie, the owner who had helped her when she'd bought the items, said the truck was already loaded and she would tell them to make Ally's house their first stop and not to forget to take her old sofa with them when they left. With her mother's voice in her head, Ally gave the old sofa a once-over to make sure it was relatively clean. Other than a few cat hairs, she was happy to see it was in decent shape, and this reminded her to be sure to cover the new sofa and chair with something, at least temporarily.

By ten thirty that morning, the truck was already leaving with her old sofa. Ally found two quilts in a closet and covered both pieces. She could simply remove them when she has company. Lucky was worth it. By eleven o'clock she was ready to call Mrs. Morgan. She knew from the 843 area code that she was in South Carolina. Mrs. Morgan answered on the first ring. She sobbed as soon as she heard Ally's voice. Even though Ally didn't know Katie very well, she was still a connection to her daughter from when she was still alive. Ally expressed how very sorry she was for the Morgans' loss. She asked if there was anything she could do to help. "Actually," said Mrs. Morgan, "there is one very big thing you can do." She asked if Ally could find the girls Katie had roomed with when she'd gone missing. She thought one of them might hold the key to finding her daughter's killer.

Ally said she would, of course, do her best, but that it might be difficult to find women from thirty years ago who have probably married and changed their names or moved out of the area entirely. Mrs. Morgan begged her to at least try. She said she knew their first names because Katie had told her a little about her roommates and of course the police had questioned all of them at the time, but this long afterwards she had no idea where they might be, and the police were having difficulty digging up records from thirty years ago. The Morgans had even hired a private investigator when the police had come up with nothing, but that too had failed to produce anything helpful. Mrs. Morgan reminded Ally of what she already knew, that Katie had been their only daughter. Apparently, they had two sons who'd been teenagers when Katie went missing, but the family had few recollections of Katie's college life. "You see," said Mrs. Morgan quietly, "when you don't even have a trail to go down, you grasp at anything you can."

Before they said goodbye, Ally promised to try and find at least one of Katie's roommates. She felt such empathy for Mrs. Morgan that she could not refuse to help her. She mentally reviewed her 'to do' list, and thought about all she'd managed to accomplish, from the new furniture to the washer/dryer to the vet appointment to having internet service installed and even landing a job! Next week she would check out the workout center that Mary had told her about. *Things were coming together nicely,* she thought with some pride.

Chapter - 8

Ally decided to call Mary and ask her if they could go to the gym together and perhaps even have lunch afterwards. Mary didn't answer so she left a message, and while she waited to hear back from her, she began thinking about how to find old yearbooks from Syracuse University. She hadn't kept any of her college yearbooks. They just gathered dust, after all, and she remembered thinking, *I don't want anyone to have to spend time tossing out a bunch of stuff after I'm gone.* She recalled her mother having to come up to New York on several trips just to clean out her grandmother's house. Ally refused to be a burden to anyone in that way.

It occurred to her that as a Syracuse University alumnus, she probably had access to old yearbooks. She had always kept up her alumni dues and even made a Christmas donation to the Alumni Club each year. Sure enough, she quickly found the alumni site online and was able to locate nursing school yearbooks. Fortunately, nursing school students had all stayed in one dormitory: Adams Hall. Katie was a year behind her so she would have been a junior in '91, the year she went missing. Nursing programs had to adapt over the years to things like population growth, shifting opportunities for women and demand for nurses, so the nursing school at Syracuse had gone from two years to four over the span of about forty years. Today, they even have a Nurse Practitioner program, which states are beginning to recognize in the Health Provider discipline.

Ally looked at each picture in the yearbook for the entering freshman class. She found Katie, of course, but since the pictures were alphabetical, she had no idea how to find her roommates, so she searched for other clues. The dormitory rooms housed four to a room. Each room had their own bathroom, which was a definite plus. Most of the time, you kept the same roommates for all four years, unless someone dropped out, moved to another house or apartment or there were personality conflicts. Snoring was not an excuse to move, you just had to cope. Ally lived on the floor above Katie's but they shared the same stairwell, so she saw her often. She searched through the book until she was blue in the face, but had no luck, so she decided to leave it alone for a while and go sit on the back porch.

Just as she was nodding off into a nap, Gene called. He sounded pleased she had accepted his job offer. He told her she would need black slacks and a crisp white blouse. He said the one she had on the other day would be fine. *He remembered?* He told her she would be given a vest to wear at the venue and suggested comfortable shoes but no sneakers. Flats would be fine. Since this would be her first time, he would pair her with Eliza so she could learn the ropes. "Be there at five," he instructed. He said he would text her the address so there would be no confusion. He also assured her that this job would be fairly easy; it was a retirement party for the president of the local hospital and would be very organized so she should not have any problems with the guests. "They don't tend to overdrink, which is not always the case at some of our other events," he admitted.

Ally was so excited when she hung up that she immediately went to her closet and pulled out a slim fitting pair of pants. She ironed her Talbot's blouse *(he remembered!)* and found a pair of black flats that she often wore to casual events in New York. All in all, she felt she would be well dressed and look professional. She forgot to ask about jewelry but decided less is more so she would simply wear her pearl earrings and nothing more.

Mary called and asked if she was free to go to the gym now and the timing was perfect, since Ally wanted to clear her mind and thought a workout would help. Mary picked her up about fifteen minutes later in her Lexus. Ally complimented her on the car.

"I bought it after Tom passed. I couldn't bear to keep driving the same car we'd shared for so many years."

When they arrived, Mary told the front desk that Ally was new and asked if they could get a tour, so a very sweet girl named Courtney came out to show them around. Ally was particularly interested in the pool and Courtney told her how the classes worked. She said there was a waiting list right now but she would put her on it and promised her that it moved pretty fast. Ally decided right then and there to join, even skipping the free two-week trial. The two new friends did a short workout on the treadmill and then stopped for lunch at a cute little deli. They agreed to try to go to the gym every Monday, Wednesday and Friday morning at seven o'clock.

"This is my kind of place," Ally said about the deli as she enjoyed her delicious salad. "There are so many delicatessens in New York, but my favorite were the Jewish ones. The pastrami and corned beef sandwiches were to die for and believe me you could die from eating all that!" She laughed loudly. As noisy as it was in there, she noticed that she got a few looks.

"I have a wonderful bookstore to take you to," said Mary as they were finishing. "You'll love it."

Azio Books was in a little house the owner had remodeled inside and was stocked with books and records. There seemed to be a wide selection. Ally found three paperbacks, but didn't buy any records because she didn't have a record player. But now she was considering buying one, if only to come back and comb through all the albums. "Well, that was a nice diversion, and a great way to end the afternoon," she remarked. "Thank you, Mary! I needed that."

When Mary dropped her off, Ally invited her over the following night to celebrate her new job. "I'll make a charcuterie board with appetizers, sound good? Come around five-thirty." Mary promised to bring dessert.

Chapter - 9

Back at home, Ally decided the task at hand was to revisit the yearbooks and try to identify at least one of Katie's roommates. A daunting task, she knew, but she wanted to do everything she could to help Mrs. Morgan. First, she opened her laptop to find out if there was anything new on the case. Apparently the police were asking for help from the public, and asked that anyone with information that could prove useful contact the Brunswick County Sheriff's office, and provided their phone number.

Ally suddenly realized she had not checked her Facebook page since she'd gotten internet service. She updated her profile and decided to take a new profile picture of herself on the beach the next time she was there. In the meantime, she snapped a picture of Lucky on a sofa pillow looking up at her sweetly and uploaded that as her profile picture, then she started reading through the posts. She saw her ex-boyfriend Gabe's postings of his children. Apparently little Sophia had just had a birthday party. She hated that she'd forgotten to send a gift.

When she and Gabe had parted ways, she felt guilty because she'd become close to the children and did not know whether to keep in touch with them or not. She decided it needed to be a clean break so he could move on as well. But now she was having doubts. She would at least send Sophia a belated birthday card with some cash in it to make up for forgetting. The children should not suffer in a break-up. Maybe they'd think of her in her old age, she thought, but then she realized how selfish that sounded.

She went back to scrolling through the posts. It took a while to go through the friend requests, but she finally finished reading everything and making the expected comments and adding emojis where appropriate. She was becoming weary of social media and all the time it took – one might even say *wasted*. She did believe it had its uses, of course: she could troll old boyfriends, for example, which could be fun when you've had a couple glasses of wine.

It occurred to her to check whether there was any social media information about Katie, even though Facebook did not exist when she went missing. Many Kathryn and Katie Morgans came up, but there was nothing that looked obvious. Apparently, there was a pop star with the same name and there were multiple pictures of her. It appeared to be a dead end. She then returned to the yearbooks she'd found yesterday, going through pictures and letting her mind relax enough to visualize how the dorm had looked all those years ago, as far as she could remember. She wondered if hypnosis could help but had no idea where to get it or who would perform it. She decided to keep that option in the back of her mind, though. She kept at it for the better part of an hour. All of a sudden, she remembered one of the girls in a picture on the activities page for the dorm. It was Fall Festival Day and each floor had been decorated for fall and Halloween. In the picture, Katie was posing with two other girls and they looked as though they knew each other well and were having a good time.

Luckily, all their names were printed under the picture. Katie was in the middle. On her left was a girl named Carmen Baxter; on her right was Cheryl Walters. Ally remembered both of them and googled their names, but got a long list of matches in response. It would take hours, if not days, to go through each one and even then she might not find the right person. She decided to contact the Alumni Association to see if they could be of help. She found a phone number for Robert Shelton, President and left him a voicemail explaining the reason for her call. She hoped for a quick response, but it was not to be.

She knew Mrs. Morgan would be waiting to hear from her, so she called and told her she'd found two possible people who could have roomed with Katie. Mrs. Morgan was ecstatic and wanted to know who they were. Ally gave her the names, but she didn't recognize either of them. Ally asked if Katie's roommates had been interviewed at the time of the disappearance. Mrs. Morgan said they had but all the police got from them was that they knew Katie was seeing someone, but they had no idea who and that they'd seen her get into a Jaguar one day. They never asked her about it and she hadn't shared anything. They'd said Katie was very secretive about who she was seeing.

"Did Katie ever tell you about anyone she was seeing?" asked Ally.

"No, she had a boyfriend over the summer and they promised to see each other over Christmas break, at least that's what I remember. He came to the vigil we held the week after the students returned from Thanksgiving break. He seemed as shocked as the rest of us, and the police questioned him and told us he wasn't a suspect."

Ally told her she was going to try to get more information from the Alumni Association president and promised to let her know if she learned anything. She didn't mention that she had a nagging feeling she knew how to reach Carmen Baxter. Ally had dated a Sigma Nu fraternity brother named Ray Baxter at the beginning of her sophomore year. She vaguely remembered him mentioning that he had a sister who'd started nursing school that same year. He would be easier to locate, so she did another Google search and narrowed the search to Syracuse University. Right away a Ray Baxter came up on Facebook and LinkedIn, along with a picture, so she knew it was the right guy. His LinkedIn said he was an attorney practicing in Albany, NY.

Five minutes later she had his receptionist on the line. Mr. Baxter was in court but she would have him return the call. *Another lead that may or may not materialize*, thought Ally glumly. Then, out of sudden curiosity, she decided to do a search of missing people in the United States. She was stunned by the results. According to the NCIC, National Crime Information Center, 93,718 people who were reported missing in 2021. Wow, she had no idea!

Ally realized she had never given it much thought beyond hearing about the ones that made headlines, like Elizabeth Smart, or the ones whose bodies were found, like Laci Peterson and JonBenet Ramsey. *How frightening it must be to have a loved one simply vanish,* she thought. Only a few were ever recovered. She felt even more energized to help the Morgan family after reading about the statistics.

Chapter - 10

Friday morning, Ally decided to start cleaning and purging. She washed every bed sheet and curtain in the house. She cleaned and scoured both bathrooms. She knew they needed updating but she had more pressing matters to deal with. After vacuuming every floor and carpet, she mopped the floors, which left the whole place a lovely pine scent. She opened the windows to get the sea breeze gently blowing through the musty house.

She had to get to Publix to pick up some meats and cheeses for the charcuterie board she'd promised Mary for that evening. Her cooking and entertaining skills were woefully inadequate so she'd watched a YouTube video on how to create a nice board. She hoped the catering job would help her improve her abilities a bit. She would also pick up a bottle of chardonnay and Prosecco at Publix, since she hadn't yet found a wine store nearby.

Just as she was leaving, the president of the Alumni Association returned her call. She explained again the reason she was reaching out and he said he knew about Katie's remains being found because the media had reported that she'd been a student at Syracuse at the time of her disappearance. More importantly, he said he'd be happy to help. He would text her the most recent addresses and phone numbers he had in their database for Cheryl Walters and Carmen Baxter. He wished her and the Morgan family well. She asked if he thought either of the women would be upset that he'd given out their contact information, but he assured her that alumni waive confidentiality when they join the club and provide their contact information, so she shouldn't worry.

Another lucky break - when she returned from shopping, Ray Baxter called. He was happy to hear from her and asked how she was. They exchanged the usual pleasantries about family and jobs and then Ally got to the point. She explained that a missing woman's remains had just been found and that she'd been a nursing student at Syracuse while they were both there. She said she remembered him mentioning when they were dating in 1989 that he had a sister who'd started nursing school that year, the same year the missing girl, Katie Morgan, had started. She explained that she'd become a bit involved in helping the family find out more about her disappearance in 1991.

Ray said he remembered his sister Carmen telling him about one of her roommates disappearing, but he and Ally were no longer dating by then. She asked if his sister could be the one in the picture she'd found in a yearbook with Katie and he said the dates were right and that he doubted there was another Carmen Baxter in the nursing school at that time. She asked if he could put her in touch with Carmen. Ray sighed and said, "If I could, I would, Ally, but unfortunately Carmen passed away three years ago from breast cancer."

Ally expressed how sorry she was to hear that and extended her sincere condolences. Ray thanked her and wished her the best with her search. "Let me know if there is anything else I can do, okay?" he said before they said goodbye.

More and more, Ally was being reminded of how precious life was. She knew as a nurse that there were still plenty of women today being diagnosed and succumbing to breast cancer. And Carmen had even been a nurse, but Ally had always maintained that nurses are less likely to take care of themselves because they consider themselves the caregivers.

Just then, Robert Shelton, the Alumni Association president, texted her the contact information for Cheryl and Carmen. Clearly their records were not up to date, since Carmen had died three years ago, but she appreciated him being so prompt. She put the investigation aside for the time being, though, so she could prepare for Mary's visit. She couldn't wait to show off her new sofa and chair, and knew they would have a fun night. As hard as it was, she managed to put Katie and Carmen out of her mind for a few hours.

Mary arrived carrying a dish of lemon bars. Ally thanked her and told her it was one of her favorites. "Please don't let me eat more than one," she joked.

The new friends relaxed and told each other about their early lives over a few glasses of wine and the delicious cheeses and meats Ally had bought. Mary said she'd grown up in a wealthy family in Greenwich, Connecticut. Her father owned multiple businesses, mostly dealing with shopping malls. Her mother came from old money just like Ally's did, but Mary's sounded like it was a lot of old money. They'd lived in a mansion.

"I was in high school when Martha Moxley was murdered in Greenwich. Do you remember that case? She was fifteen and her body was found the day after Halloween. She'd been killed with a golf club. Michael Skakel, who was a nephew of Ethel Kennedy, was a suspect, along with his brother, but Michael was eventually tried and convicted."

Ally was amazed that Mary had lived so close to where this famous murder had taken place. "Were you ever questioned about anything?" she wanted to know.

"No, I was not a friend of hers and was two years behind her in school. My brother, Harry, was in her class, but he was out of town when the murder occurred. He was part of the Lacrosse team. The investigation was very low profile because of the connection to the Kennedys, and if her mother and a journalist whose name I've forgotten had not stayed on it, I don't think it ever would have been solved."

The Kennedy curse, thought Ally.

Chapter - 11

Ally awoke the next morning with a slight headache. She was not accustomed to mixing her wines, and figured it was the Prosecco's fault. She and Mary had had a great time last night sharing the Italian meats and cheeses, and Mary's lemon squares proved a perfect balance after the rich foods. They'd topped it all off with a delicious Guatemalan coffee she'd found at Aldi's, of all places. She was relaxing in bed with Lucky when there was a knock at the door. She looked at the clock and was startled to find it was much later than she'd thought.

It turned out it was only FedEx delivering a package. She noticed the Syracuse return address and when she opened it, she smiled. Robert Shelton had sent her copies of the yearbooks of the nursing school from 1990 through 1992, along with a note: *"Hope these will help you find what you need. Good luck and God Bless You, Robert."*

Now she could keep perusing yearbooks for more clues.

She had her first catering job later that day, so she wanted to get some much-needed exercise while she still had the energy. She threw on her comfortable capris and an SU sweatshirt, fed Lucky, put on her old walking shoes, and walked to the beach, which was deserted at the moment. She decided to do a short run but was careful because it had been a long time since she'd run, and the last thing she wanted on her first day of work were leg cramps or foot issues. Her legs were going to be very important in her job. She spotted the shrimp boats in the distance and thought how the pandemic had taken away a lot but not people's appetites for good food.

When she'd gone back to walking, she saw a man coming toward her. Judging from his physique and his graying hair, he seemed to be about sixty, though appeared to be in excellent condition. She wondered briefly if he was a runner. Maybe he'd noticed her running earlier.

As he got closer, he smiled and asked, pointing to her sweatshirt, "Did you go to Syracuse University?"

"Yes, you too?"

He said he'd graduated in '85. They stood there awkwardly staring at each other for a second until Ally broke the ice with, "How long have you lived here?"

"Well, I only come down on weekends. I have a home in Raleigh and I'm still working. I hope to retire in about seven years."

Ally nodded, then shared, "I'm here permanently now. I was a nurse in New York City but was laid off when I refused the vaccine." She was surprised at herself for offering so much information to someone she'd just met, but something about him made her feel at ease. Usually when she told her story, people just said it was too bad and went on their way, but he looked her square in the eye and said how sorry he was and that it seemed like a courageous thing to do. Ally felt an immediate connection and something told her not to walk away.

"My name is Neal. Neal Smith. I'm actually a doctor, so I feel your pain, no pun intended," he smirked. "I work in Chapel Hill as an anesthesiologist. I took the vaccine and the boosters but I regret it. At the time we weren't being pressured but everyone was lining up for it so I just went along. Fortunately, I haven't had any ill effects."

They walked together down the beach as if they'd been together all along. Ally suddenly realized she hadn't introduced herself. "I'm Ally, short for Allison, Malcom." She asked him point blank if he was married because she would feel funny if his wife were to show up out of the blue, but he said he was divorced and had been for a very long time. He had one son who was a dentist in Pinehurst, NC.

"Lucky me, I have a place to stay when I want to go play golf." He chuckled and she did too. She sensed he liked her and wanted to get to know her better.

"Do you do anything for recreation while you're here on the island?" she asked, curious if he was in a relationship or had other places to be.

"Nope, I just come down every other weekend or so, especially in nice weather, and work on the house. I've purposely not made too many friends since I'm here so infrequently. I have neighbors who'll occasionally ask me over for lunch or dinner if they see me. There are many of us who have homes elsewhere because we're still in the game of pursuing the 'dream'," he said with a wink.

He asked if she would like to have a drink or have lunch with him sometime. He said he'd be around until Monday afternoon but was expected back on rotation on Tuesday. She said she was tied up that day but that maybe they could meet for lunch tomorrow. It sounded like a question. He smiled and said that would be great. He suggested the Oyster Rock in Calabash but then remembered they were closed for lunch.

"How about dinner instead?" he suddenly suggested.

"Okay, sure, I can do dinner," Ally found herself agreeing. They made a date to meet at Oyster Rock at five o'clock the next day. As she walked back to her house, she turned to make sure he was not following… you just never knew. Then she chided herself for being so suspicious of such a lovely man.

As soon as she got home, she Googled Dr. Neal Smith in Chapel Hill and his complete vitae popped up along with a Facebook page. She reviewed his Facebook page but there had not been any posts on it for three years.

That evening she arrived at the Southport Convention Center at four forty-five, as instructed. She found her way around to the back door and saw the Three Island Catering truck. Gene saw her and waved her over. He introduced her to Eliza, who then showed her the set up from the kitchen to the ballroom. She explained they would each have their own section. She told Ally she should watch her for a while and then she would be let loose once she was comfortable with knowing what to do.

Eliza made a point of telling Ally that Gene was very particular and to remember that the patron, or diner, whichever she chose to call them, is always right. Ally knew she was trying to intimidate her but it's difficult to intimidate someone who's been responsible for a patient with tubes in every orifice, knowing you must check everything every fifteen minutes. Try that, Eliza! Ally thought with a wry little smile.

The patrons started arriving at six o'clock. They were greeted with a glass of Prosecco, then shown to their table as a trio played soft background music. It didn't appear this would be a very rowdy crowd, thought Ally, just as Gene had surmised. Everyone was cordial and she was slowly getting the hang of moving through her assigned group of tables. The appetizers were on the table, the salads were being brought out and Eliza seemed to be settling down and even smiling at times.

The entrees had been served but there was one misstep in her group. A lovely lady whispered to Ally that she had requested gluten-free. Ally assured her that she would handle it and within two minutes she had placed the correct dish in front of the woman, who thanked her with an appreciative smile.

The emcee announced some special guests and another forty-five minutes was spent with speeches and accolades, apparently well-deserved for the honored guest. It seemed the president of the local hospital was retiring and the speeches were very moving. Dessert was passed out towards the end of the speeches. After dessert the trio of musicians piped up and began playing swing music. The patrons started "cutting a rug," as Ally's grandparents used to describe dancing.

Ally was fairly exhausted by the end of the evening. She stayed and helped lug some of the equipment out to the van. She knew that wasn't included in her job description but she wanted to do her part and hopefully make a good impression. Apparently, it worked, because Eliza told her she'd passed and said she'd be on her own in the future.

Chapter - 12

Ally woke Sunday morning to a meowing Lucky. She'd gotten in late last night and hoped he hadn't thought he'd been deserted. His litter box was full, so she fed him (or her) and then thoroughly cleaned it out, replacing the litter.

Sunday was the one day she liked to gorge on breakfast. She had childhood memories of her dad making waffles and sausage or bacon every Sunday. She'd switched to turkey bacon a while back but still enjoyed making waffles so she dug out her grandmother's old waffle iron and, to her amazement, it still worked. She shared part of her waffle with Lucky, who was happy to have some human food.

She figured it was a good time to do some weeding in the small yard out front. She had hired a lawn service to mow but the flower bed still needed weeding. She worked up a sweat in the hot sun, but before showering she decided to go for a beach walk to get her day off to a good start. She begrudgingly put on her old ASICS running shoes, but made a mental note to get a new pair. The beach was crowded with umbrellas as far as the eye could see in both directions, but at least the sand was nice and clean. She noticed the tire tracks from the turtle patrol. That made her think about poor Katie's body being found.

Once she got home, she pulled out the yearbooks again, but then remembered that Robert had texted her Cheryl Walter's address and phone number. She hoped it was current, but decided to hold off calling until after noon, in case Cheryl was a church-goer.

She used her time to do more unpacking, an unpleasant task that she'd been procrastinating on, and pulled out a few boxes from the spare bedroom. She found her old nurse's hat well preserved in tissue and a plastic bag. Oh, how they'd all hated wearing those hats. In a way it was an object of pride but the impracticality of wearing them had gradually weaned them out. The poor nursing students still had to wear them on duty. Ally even found her diploma that she'd never bothered framing. Before she knew it, it was nearly twelve-thirty. She mused about how time flew when you found yourself reminiscing.

She dialed the 404 area code, which she knew was an Atlanta number. A woman answered and Ally was relieved to not have another delay in her quasi-sleuthing. She asked for Cheryl Walters, and the woman said she was Cheryl. Ally explained how she'd gotten her number and they exchanged a few pleasantries before Ally got to the point.

"Oh, wow, I haven't heard that name in years," said Cheryl when Ally asked about Katie Morgan. Ally had to break the news that Katie's remains had been washed up on the beach in NC. Cheryl took a moment to digest this information and maybe even to say a prayer. Ally waited quietly and once she thought Cheryl was ready to talk, she asked her if she had been one of Katie's roommates.

"Yes, we roomed together freshman and sophomore years. We had just started our third year together when she went missing." She confirmed that Carmen Baxter was another of their roommates but said Carmen had passed away a few years ago. Ally didn't tell her she knew that already because she didn't want to sound like she's been digging around. Instead, she led the conversation to what they'd all told the police at the time.

"I only remember telling them we hadn't seen her for about two days but hadn't even realized it because it was such a busy time, with Thanksgiving and exams coming up and all."

Ally asked her if she remembered anything about Katie dating someone and if they'd really seen her get into a Jaguar with a man.

Cheryl sighed, then said softly, "I have to admit we were pretending to be helpful and lied about that to impress the police. I felt terrible about it afterwards, but didn't have the courage to tell them we'd lied." She said she knew it was an awful thing to have done to mislead the police like that and has asked for forgiveness in her prayers many times. But at the time, they had no idea Katie wouldn't just turn up again with some excuse for taking off. She almost wrote to Katie's mother to confess but then lost her courage. She sounded very remorseful so Ally didn't press too hard and tried not to sound judgmental. She thought, *after all these years, what good would it do anyway?*

But now she realized that Cheryl and Carmen were both a dead end. Cheryl couldn't even remember the name of their other roommate, since she'd only lived with them for a little while. She remembered she was Jewish and was dating a non-Jewish boy her parents did not approve of. They were always having to sneak around so none of her friends would see them together. That was all Cheryl could tell Ally. She promised she would call if she remembered anything more that could be helpful. Ally also gave her the Brunswick County Sheriff's telephone number. Disappointed, she wanted to talk about all of it with someone, and thought of Mary. She called to see if she was up for a walk along the beach and Mary was happy to join her.

They walked to the beach and headed west. Ally decided to unload on Mary. She told her the entire story, from finding out about the identity of the remains and contacting Mrs. Morgan, who now lived with her husband in North Myrtle Beach. She told her about the disappointing dead ends and said she felt a kinship with Katie's mom and wanted to help her.

"Would bones hold up in salt water all that time?"

"Good question," said Ally, "I think they theorized she'd been tied up in a tarp or some other kind of protective material and that kept the bones from breaking down or from sea creatures getting at them."

"Do you think she was in the water all those years?"

"Who knows?" said Ally with a shrug. "Do you think the police would tell me anything, since I'm not family?"

"Probably not. But maybe you could try the coroner's office in Wilmington or Raleigh. They might be able to tell how long she was in the water, which could narrow down when she was killed and dumped. Then there's the question of where she was put in the water," Mary said thoughtfully.

"I hadn't thought of that," said Ally. "I think the police thought she was either kidnapped or disappeared of her own free will in Syracuse, but as far as I know they never found any clues. The Syracuse Police Department didn't have anything to go on back then, from what I understand, and on top of that, now I know they were misled by Katie's roommates. It's possible I have more information than they do at this point," said Ally.

When they'd exhausted the grim subject of Katie Morgan, Ally changed the subject and told Mary about meeting Dr. Neal Smith and the dinner plans they had made for that night. Mary was very happy for her, and said she couldn't wait to hear more, but reminded Ally to be a little cautious of someone she'd just met. Ally agreed, but was nevertheless excited to see where the evening led.

Chapter - 13

When Ally got home, she decided to call Mrs. Morgan to fill her in on her conversation with Cheryl Walters. She revealed that Carmen and Cheryl had lied to the police about seeing Katie getting into a Jaguar because they wanted to seem helpful and that Cheryl felt terrible about it but never contacted the police to change her story. In fairness, Ally offered, they'd thought at the time that Katie had just gone off somewhere to be alone and would return on her own.

"I just cannot believe they would do that," Mrs. Morgan said, sounding disappointed and deflated.

To change the subject, Ally said, "I was wondering if we could meet somewhere to brainstorm and figure out if there are any other clues we could follow.''

Mrs. Morgan thought that was a wonderful idea and suddenly perked up at the prospect of having someone help her find out what had happened to her only daughter. The police, after all, weren't sharing much information and she hated having to keep calling them. She asked Ally if she would mind coming to North Myrtle Beach? They agreed on ten o'clock the following morning.

After they'd said goodbye, Ally combed through her closet to find an appropriate outfit for her dinner date. Since she'd moved to NC in a bit of a hurry, she hadn't had a chance to do much clothes shopping. She

Googled the Oyster Rock to get an idea of how to dress and to see what kind of food to expect. She was impressed.

She felt a simple sundress would be appropriate to the laid back atmosphere of the beach, but she tried to find a shawl or something to match, knowing it could be a little cooler at night in April. She picked out a navy and white sundress, cut a little low in front but she at least she could still wear a full bra because of the wide straps. She found a silk white wrap to throw over her shoulders. Her navy colored Mephisto slides with a slight heel would round out the outfit perfectly.

To calm her nerves while she got dressed, she had a tequila shot. She was pleased to see that she'd gotten a little sun on her arms and legs and looked much less like a vacationer from the north. Her dark brown hair had some sun streaks in it, too. All in all, she thought she looked pretty fetching. A word her grandfather Elias would have used on her. How she missed her grandparents.

She arrived just after five and found Neal waiting out front. He looked nervous, she thought. As soon as he saw her, he smiled warmly and his blue eyes lit up. It did not hurt that he was wearing a light blue Untuckit shirt. He had on white shorts and dockers. Very casual indeed. She hoped he didn't think she was overdressed.

They sat at a lovely table in the corner, from which they could see the entire marina and beyond. He asked what kind of wine she liked. Then he blushed and said a little apologetically, "I guess I assumed you drank alcohol." Ally assured him she enjoyed wine and said any kind would be fine with her, though she preferred chardonnay.

He ordered a very expensive bottle of Jordan Chardonnay, 2019 vintage. He also ordered an appetizer of crab dip after making sure she was a fan of crab dips. They spoke of their years at SU. He'd done his undergraduate there and then attended the University of NC at Chapel Hill for medical school, and that's where he ended up staying. He'd married his girlfriend from college, but she'd had a difficult time adjusting: first, to living in the south and second, to his schedule once he was working full time. They made a go of it, especially since they had a son, but they eventually grew apart and decided to go their separate ways. They'd divorced in 2007 and she initially moved back to Syracuse but got tired of the weather and didn't really know anyone there anymore, so she'd moved to California to be near her brother and his family.

By the time he'd finished his life story, it was time to order dinner. They both ordered the grouper. Neal assured her it was the best thing on the menu and Ally discovered he was right. As they ate, she shared with him the highlights of her life. He already knew about her losing her job so she told him about her parents and their move to Bartow, Florida.

She told him about her brother, Craig, and his career in Tampa, in sports medicine, and said her sister, Janet, and her husband had moved to Texas many years ago and were parents to Ally's only niece and nephew. That was about the extent of her family, she said. She had a cousin on her father's side but never saw them. She also told him about inheriting, sort of, the house she was currently living in. "It's nice to have options when you need them," she said with a smile.

He told her he'd bought a house during the '08 economic downturn and got lucky. He'd bought it from a builder who was going under, so it was not completed but needed mostly cosmetic finishes, which he knew he could do himself or hire out. "It was a great investment at the time," he said, "but I haven't used it very much." He said it was in need of some serious redecorating, but he wanted to do as much of the remodeling as he could by himself..

"You and me both… with the houses, I mean," she joked, and they both laughed.

"My father was a woodworker and made beautiful cabinets," he told her. "I'm afraid I didn't get that gene but I do enjoy using a skill saw and doing drywall, things like that."

Ally shook her head. "I wouldn't know where to begin. I never even considered doing any of my own work. I've lived in an apartment for so many years and you just call the super when anything breaks."

"Well, as you get older, you rethink a lot of things," Neal told her.

Ally wondered if he was thinking about running into her on the beach when out of the blue he said, "Let's go for a walk along the water."

Ally tried to pay half the bill, but he waved her off adamantly and paid. Then they walked along the boardwalk that went around a small cove at the tip of where the restaurant ended. There was an outside Oyster Bar at the end, which was very crowded. The sky was clear and the moon was very bright, even though it was only a half- moon.

"Do you know much about Calabash?" asked Neal, referring to the town they were in.

"No, not really."

"Well, the folklore here is that Jimmy Durante enjoyed eating at one of these local restaurants so much that as he was leaving he turned to the woman who owned the restaurant and said 'Goodnight, Mrs. Calabash.' Then when he had a TV show in the sixties he began ending every show with that as a tip of his hat to her, adding 'wherever you are."

"True story?" asked Ally.

"Well, I think at some later point he finally revealed that he was referring to a nickname for his first wife, and he added 'wherever you are' after she died, but it's a nice little legend for the town, don't you think?" He laughed.

Ally was really enjoying herself and decided to avoid the Katie story for now. She didn't want to bring the conversation down with such a heavy subject, but she also didn't want to put Neal off by making him think she had all this 'baggage.' After all, she hardly knew him! They went back inside and had an after-dinner cup of coffee at the bar. He walked her to her car and said he would love to call her when he was down again if she would allow him to. They pulled out their cell phones and exchanged numbers. She thanked him for a lovely evening. She extended her hand to shake hands but he pulled her into an embrace and they kissed lightly, then he waited for her to drive off before walking to his car.

Chapter - 14

Ally awoke around eight o'clock, later than she'd planned. She knew it would take her about thirty-five minutes to get to the Morgans in North Myrtle Beach, so she quickly showered and put on her jeans and a loose cream- colored top. She fed Lucky and quickly cleaned the litter box, then managed a quick cup of coffee and a half a grapefruit before heading out. Traffic was busier than she was used to but luckily she arrived around nine-fifty. *Better early than late*, she thought, hearing her mother's voice in her head.

She forgot to call in to work to find out if she would be needed that day but she had her cell so they could reach her if necessary.

Mrs. Morgan greeted her at the door. She said her husband had a prearranged golf game so he wouldn't be able to join them and apologized.

"Oh, please don't apologize, Mrs. Morgan. I understand," responded Ally. Ally assessed the older woman. She was a petite woman in her mid-seventies, maybe five-one with a large bust but small hips and legs. She was wearing a pair of khaki pants and a light yellow knit sweater. She had a lovely Celtic cross around her neck. Ally commented on the cross and she told her she'd bought it on a trip to Ireland a few years earlier.

"I wish I could have bought one for Katie. We have Irish blood, at least according to 23andMe," she smiled sheepishly. "Please call me Marie and my husband is Larry," she said.

"I have to tell you that I found something recently in the attic that may be of interest," she began without preamble as Ally followed her into the living room. "It is a letter from a person named Anna. The letter has no return address and was postmarked October 29th. I found it in a box in the attic that Larry had used when he cleaned out his office desk before we moved. He doesn't remember getting it, but guesses he just picked up the mail and held it in his desk with the intention of giving it to Katie when we would be there at Thanksgiving. He normally would have handed it to me, but it was possible that I was out and he may have been in a hurry and just threw it in his desk drawer with other stuff. He would have been so upset when Katie went missing, he thinks he just forgot about it and over the years it got pushed to the bottom of his pile of stuff he collected but never got to, kind of like my kitchen junk drawer. He is a procrastinator and waited until the last minute to clean out his desk before we moved from Doylestown, just outside of Philly. The letter was amongst the pile of stuff he never seemed to get to. It has been in that box for seventeen years."

She handed the letter to Ally. "Katie was supposed to come home for the Thanksgiving holiday that year. She would have been home on that Wednesday before Thanksgiving, but she went missing on the 9th, two weeks before Thanksgiving. The letter must have arrived around the 1st of November The police came to our house and asked to search Katie's room and of course, we allowed them to do so. Anything we could do to help find her we would have done. The spent about an hour going through her room, every drawer, her closet, everything." If only Larry had remembered there was a letter. Grief and fear absolutely paralyze one in times like these. We barely got through it but we had two sons to raise so we soldiered on, as the British would say."

Dear Katie,

I wanted to thank you again for the $3,000 you gave to help us *get this apartment and have enough to live here until I can come up with a plan. Mrs. Lee has been the kindest woman. She fixes us food without me asking. She loves the children so much. She said she never had children and her husband died ten years ago. She told me we could stay as long as I liked for a nominal monthly rent. She will pay our utility bills and does not expect to be reimbursed. I've been able to go out each day looking for a job.*

I don't have very nice outfits to wear for interviews but Mrs. Lee has a friend who knows about an organization that receives clothing donations for battered women's shelters to help them dress to find jobs. They even help with resumes and coach them to help them in their interviews. She said so many of the women are self-conscious about their circumstances, and this makes it difficult to convince an employer to hire them. There are many hurdles to jump.

Having children is another but Mrs. Lee is helping me with that, too. She is happy to look after the children anytime. She works with both girls on their education. We enrolled Caroline in 3rd grade at the local elementary school. The school is aware of the situation and will contact me if her father shows up. Mrs. Lee takes her to school and picks her up every day. My little Monica has really come out of her shell. She asks about you all the time. I have to tell her you will be in touch soon. I know it's not true but she is not aware of time yet so maybe she'll see you in a year or so and that will be soon enough. Baby Joey is the same. He coos and is getting fat with Mrs. Lee's wonderful cooking. I have to watch how many snacks she gives him!

I hope you get this letter when you arrive home for your Thanksgiving holiday with your family. Just know how much your sacrifice has meant to us and that there is a special place in heaven for you.

Much love,

Anna

Chapter - 15

Katie

I arrived at school for my junior year on September 8, 1991. It was a Sunday. Classes were to start on Tuesday. Nursing students were expected to be in a general meeting on Monday. I was so excited to see Cheryl and Carmen. We had roomed together the first two years. We had a new roommate: Rennie Schwartz. She was from Long Island, some town I couldn't even pronounce. She was nice but not as friendly as Cheryl and Carmen. She may have just felt left out, since we all knew each other.

My mother had driven me up from outside of Philly, a small town I grew up in and loved. I had to say goodbye to my summer love, Brad, who was headed back to Penn State. We had a great time all summer while we were working at the local Sears. We made all of the usual promises: "I will write to you every day and we'll see each other during Thanksgiving break." Well, we knew the first promise would be broken quickly but there was a possibility the second one would be kept.

Mom made sure I had everything I needed, including an extra $100 for emergencies. I hated to see her go but was ready to see my friends and find out what they'd been up to for the last three months. Cheryl has a serious boyfriend and is hoping for a ring by Valentine's Day. Carmen just worked at McDonald's all summer and was happy to be out of her house as much as possible. She doesn't get along with her parents very well. She seems to have a wild streak at times, to be honest.

We had our general meeting, which included all of the nursing students. They wanted to set the tone for the semester, including expectations and opportunities. They mentioned several volunteer opportunities for students. Since SU is a prominent university with all of the social problems of large cities, they're approached constantly for any help students can offer. Nursing students are expected to do more. We are told it looks good on resumes when applying for jobs. They handed out flyers that listed various opportunities. I decided I would look at them later and choose something. The first two years were stressful and I could not afford any time to do extra activities because of studying but this year I feel calmer and can probably help in some volunteer capacity.

Later that evening I remembered the flyer and looked it over. The first one I saw was called Men and Women's Reserve Shelter. Strange name, I thought. In the description, it said it takes in battered families and supports them with food and clothing. It said they need help with general duties like cleaning and cooking. They didn't distinguish between men or women but obviously, I'm guessing there are more women than men in need. I decided to call the phone number provided the next day to find out more about what they need and how involved it would be. I noticed they gave just general directions to the shelter but I knew it was on the opposite side of town. I figured they would be more specific with directions when I called. I realized they had to be careful to keep everyone safe. There were instructions on the paper to not leave it in any open area and not to give out telephone numbers.

The next day I called and told the receptionist who I was and why I was calling. She transferred me to another number and a woman named Rosie answered. She asked me several personal and what felt like unnecessary questions. She then apologized, after I guess I passed, and told me they are trained to assess each call and 'weed out the kooks'. She explained the people there were running from trouble but trouble tries to find them. This information of course scared me and I almost told her it was not for me, but for some reason I felt a nudge on my right shoulder and felt emboldened. I told her I would love to help if I could. She told me to call her on a day I knew I could visit for an interview and tour. I assured her I would.

Chapter - 16

Ally

Ally just stared at the letter. She looked at the postmark but it was faded and of no help in determining from where it had been mailed. "We need to turn this letter over to the Brunswick Sheriff's office, Detective Hernandez, do you agree?"

"Yes, I do, said Marie, but then hesitated.

"Do you really think they'll investigate a thirty-year-old case with the same energy of a more recent one?"

Ally thought she might have a point, but said, "I don't feel right not letting them know about this discovery." They made a plan to check for shelters near the university to see if they could figure out if Katie had visited or volunteered at one. Marie also knew where the $3,000 had come from that was mentioned in the letter.

"Katie's father sent her that money to purchase a used car, but we never found one and neither did the police," she said. "Nobody knew of Katie buying a car," she added with a terrible sadness in her voice.

The check had been deposited in Katie's bank account but then withdrawn on October 16th, approximately two weeks before the letter had arrived at their home. Marie said, "Katie was a responsible person and she would not have squandered her father's money unless it was for a good reason."

Ally told Marie she would go home and start searching for shelters to see what she could find out. There had to be a reason Katie gave money to this family without telling anyone. "I am going to call Detective Hernandez on my way home and make an appointment for both of us to go in with this letter. I think we can run a parallel investigation as long as we are up front with them. They can direct us as to whether or not to contact the Syracuse police. Perhaps the police departments prefer to work together.

"Oh, before I forget, a friend of mine had an idea I hadn't thought of," said Ally. "She suggested we check with the coroner's office that performed Katie's autopsy to see if they could tell how long her body had been in the water. She thought that bones disintegrate in salt water, but I told her about the news report that said it was believed Katie was wrapped in a tarp of some kind that may have slowed down decomposition. Either way, the coroner might be able to give us more information about all of that, so with your permission, I'd like to contact them to see if they'll tell me anything. It may shed more light on when she was put in the water."

"Yes, of course," Marie agreed. "I'm so grateful you're willing to help us, Ally. I hope they'll give you more information, but if you need me to call them and give my approval as the relative, please let me know."

Ally located Detective Hernandez's phone number in her recent calls and was able to make contact with her. She explained that she and Marie Morgan need to come in to see her at her earliest convenience regarding the Katie Morgan case. They made an appointment for the next morning. Ally called Marie and asked her to meet at the Brunswick Sheriff's office at the complex in Bolivia at ten o'clock in the morning. "No problem, I am bringing Larry with me," said Marie.

When Ally got home, she was so wound up she decided to take a beach walk to clear her head. She remembered the nursing school always held a general meeting the day before classes started. At that meeting they told the students about several organizations in the area that sought volunteers. They always gave out a sheet of paper with opportunities and contact information. Now she wondered if the alumni president, Robert Shelton, would be able to access archived information to see if any of this was in the college newsletter that year.

As she was washing the sand off her legs and feet, Sara from the catering company called and asked if she could work a gig at a clubhouse in Ocean Isle this coming Friday night. It was a birthday bash and wouldn't be as large as the last one, so there would only be two servers and a bartender.

"Sure,' agreed Ally.

"Great," said Sara. "It starts at seven o'clock but you need to be there by six. I'll text you the address. Oh, and wear the same uniform."

Chapter - 17

Katie

I had just one morning class the next day and wouldn't be starting my clinicals until the following day, so I called the shelter at noon and spoke with Rosie. She asked me to be there at one o'clock. I had to take a taxi, but if it worked out, I would check out the bus schedule so transportation would be cheaper.

When I arrived, the front desk assistant showed me to Rosie's office. After assessing me in person, Rosie did as she had promised and gave me a tour of the building as she explained how the facility worked, including the intake and outtake systems. We went back to her office, where she asked me about my major and what I wanted to do when I graduated. She also asked me if I had ever known or been associated with anyone who had to go to a shelter or if I knew anything about foster care. I said no and then started wondering what I was getting into.

She assured me it would be a tough but satisfying experience if I was up to it. "You'll see many things you're not used to. There is plenty of sorrow, but there is also a lot of joy. You can make of it what you want." She gave me a booklet that explained how the system worked and asked me to read it thoroughly. She said confidentiality was paramount. "Women, and some men, come here seeking asylum from an abusive spouse or partner. Abuse comes in many forms. Sometimes it is alcohol or drug-related but sometimes it is just cruelty. If there are children involved, it is more complicated." I promised to read the booklet thoroughly before deciding to become a volunteer. I said I would be back when I had another afternoon free.

I read the booklet at least five times. I got down on my knees and prayed in earnest for guidance. I could not help but think about the wonderful home my parents had made for me and my two younger brothers. My father had never raised a voice much less a hand to any of us. Of course, we had been disciplined when we misbehaved, but it usually amounted to being grounded or not being allowed to watch TV or being given extra chores around the house.

One time when I was supposed to clean my room, I decided to ride my bike to my friend's house instead. When I returned, I was sent to my room not only to clean it but also to enjoy it for the rest of the day.

Was it time for me to help others? After all, I am going into the nursing field and I feel like l have that empathetic gene. I don't want to discuss it with my roommates because I have a feeling, they'd try to talk me out of it. Am I strong enough to do this on my own, though? The truth is I believe this opportunity came about for a reason, so I think I can give it a try.

On Thursday I called Rosie and told her I could come on Friday, if that worked for her. My class would be over by noon so I'd be able to get the bus in time to be there by one. I'd checked the bus schedules and even though it required a transfer I wanted to save cab money for when I would really need it. Syracuse Transit stopped at the corner of the building where I had my last class so it was a quick walk. I would have to skip lunch but I should be back in time for dinner in the cafeteria.

When I arrived, Rosie was in a meeting with a new family that had just entered the facility. I was asked to wait outside the door to give them some privacy. I saw a very thin woman through the partially pulled blinds. She seemed nervous and was holding a baby. Two little girls were sitting together in one chair. They looked so frail and sad. About half an hour later, Rosie came out holding the girls' hands and asked me to follow them. The woman with the baby, who I assumed was their mother, followed us. We went down a hallway into a larger room that held two sets of bunk beds, a double bed and a dresser. There was no closet.

Rosie introduced me to the mother. "Katie, this is Anna." I nodded and smiled at the baby.

"This is Joey," said Anna, introducing me to her baby.

I bent down and asked the girls their names. The oldest one spoke for both of them, "My name is Caroline and this is Monica." Monica didn't speak.

I said I was happy to meet them and smiled at both of them.

This was my introduction to the system of abuse and redemption. Unfortunately, there was more of the first than the last. I took a cue from Rosie that I should play with Monica and Caroline to keep them distracted. They were quiet girls and had a hard time looking me in the eyes. I found some Barbie dolls still in the package in a nearby bin that Rosie pointed to and their eyes lit up. For the next hour they undressed and dressed the dolls, switching clothes back and forth. I enjoyed watching them. I had no sisters to play with and enjoyed watching these sisters playing with each other. Caroline was a mother hen. When it was time for me to go, they both clung to my hips and I promised them I would be back to see them soon.

Chapter - 18

Ally

Now that she had Marie Morgan's permission, Ally called the Brunswick County coroner's office to see what she could find out. They explained that Katie Morgan's remains had been sent to Fayetteville where the state lab was located and they would be handling the case. She called the number they gave her and was transferred around a few times before being told that the coroner was not available at the moment, but he would return her call when he was able. She hoped he would follow through.

She then left a voicemail for Robert Shelton, telling him she had another request and hoping he wouldn't mind. He called her back almost immediately, which surprised and impressed her. She decided to tell him the real reason she was looking for all this information.

Thankfully, Robert was sympathetic and promised to do all he could to help. "I can't believe the number of college students who go missing every year. It's awful and I often get calls from parents for help, but most of the time there's little I can do other than refer them to other sources. But," he added, "in this case I might be able to help. The school keeps an extensive file system going back many, many years. More than likely the information will be on microfiche, and if it's there, I know the person who can find it." He told her it would be two to three days, depending on how busy they were, but she should expect a call back. He wished her luck with her search.

Ally realized that it was now a waiting game, but she had no intention of giving up. She called Detective Hernandez to see if she would give Ally any updates on the case. Hernandez said she couldn't reveal much about an ongoing investigation, but she could tell her that so far there was no definitive cause of death. She said she might know more in a week or so. Ally thanked her for her time and for agreeing to share what she could, and reassured the detective that she had Marie Morgan's blessing to gather as much information as she could.

Ally knew she wouldn't hear from Neal until he returned, which could be more than a week, according to what he'd told her about his schedule, and she had no plans until the catering job on Friday night, so she decided to give Mary a call. Mary was pleased to hear from her and invited her over for dinner that night. "You've hosted twice, after all; it's my turn," she said.

She was at Mary's thirty minutes later with a bottle of chardonnay. As she approached the front door, she admired Mary's garden. She could tell Mary loved taking care of it and she had beautiful roses. Ally complimented her on her green thumb. Mary said she'd found solace in gardening after her husband died. "My biggest problem is keeping the deer away," she frowned. She said she was researching humane ways to deter them but wasn't having much luck. "I heard human hair could do it so I went to the local hair salon and asked them for a bag of hair!" They both got a good chuckle out of that.

Her front porch had lovely wicker furniture with blue striped cushions and there were pots of flowers everywhere. It was very 'Zen'-like, noted Ally to herself.

Mary had made a pineapple and strawberry tray with a delicious fruit dip. She opened the wine Ally had brought and over the wine and appetizer, Ally brought her up to date on the progress of her 'investigation.' She told her about the letter Marie had shown her and their decision to hold off on giving it to the police.

"I guess it can't hurt to wait a little while," agreed Mary.

"I also got Marie's permission to speak to the coroner and am waiting to hear back from them, but it might be a while because they're very busy."

"Have you looked into elementary schools in the area to see if you can find anything out about the oldest child?"

"Oh, good idea," nodded Ally, though wondered aloud if that would bear any fruit. "I wonder how far back their records go, plus I only have a first name."

Mary agreed it would likely be difficult, but couldn't hurt to try. Ally told her she was also waiting to hear back from the alumni association to find out if they can track down names of any organizations in the area that were asking for volunteers from the school at the time of Katie's disappearance.

They decided to change the subject to more pleasant things, so Mary asked how her date with the doctor had gone.

"He was such a gentleman," Ally smiled coyly. "We exchanged numbers and he said he'd call, so I hope he does. We seem to have a lot in common and there's just something about him that makes me want to get to know him better. He seems kind of in need of companionship, too. Anyway, that's just my opinion," she shrugged.

Mary had prepared a delicious meal of lemon chicken with fresh broccoli and orzo. She had set such a pretty table that Ally now was definitely interested in going consignment store shopping with her. Before saying goodnight, they made a date to do so on Wednesday morning when they would be fresh, then they'd have lunch out because Ally wanted to try different restaurants in the area. Ally told her she likes the 'shabby chic' style of decor because that was all she could afford right now anyway. Mary laughed knowingly and said, "Perfect," as if she already had some ideas of what to look for.

The following morning was the first real rain they'd had in weeks. Lucky was curled up beside Ally on the sofa as she turned on the news and heard the weather report warn there was a storm coming up the coast. Not quite a tropical storm but it was going to unload on the area for a while. Since the weather deterred her from going out, she decided to concentrate on emptying another box or two. She found more wine glasses and some dishes she had been looking for. Her kitchen was a nice size but the design was dated. She was not ready to do any major work on it yet but thought she might at least look into painting the cabinets white and buying new hardware. She would ask Mary what she thought, since she had interior designing experience. In the meantime, she was carefully watching her budget and hoping to get more catering jobs. She knew the season would become much busier soon, with weddings and graduations, so she would hang on to see what happened.

As she prepared a salad for lunch, Robert Shelton called. He said he had great news - his contact in archives had spent the last two days going through microfiche from the 1991 first semester and had found a newsletter with an article asking for volunteers. Amazingly, there was a name attached to the flier and, as luck would have it, that person still worked at the college, so she could likely get in touch with them. Ally realized this could be a significant breakthrough and thanked Robert profusely, who was pleased to have done something to help. The tide was turning, she thought hopefully.

She immediately called the number provided and got a voicemail for Dr. Newton's office. Ally left her cell number. She hoped this person would be willing to help her, since she was almost out of leads. Almost immediately, she received a call from an unknown number with the same area code as Syracuse. The caller said she'd received a call from this number and wondered who it was. Apparently, she hadn't listened to her voicemail.

Ally explained she had received her number from Robert Shelton and then went into further detail. "I'm looking for information on a newsletter from 1991 that listed local organizations that were seeking volunteers from SU nursing students. I know it's been a very long time and it's a long shot, but this could help solve the disappearance of a nursing student back then." She waited anxiously for a response.

There was a long silence on the line. At first Ally thought the connection had dropped but after a few more seconds, Dr. Newton said she not only remembered the newsletter but remembered the great response they'd received from it.

"I was majoring in psychology at the time and this was a public service project we'd developed. We didn't expect such an outpouring of people wanting to help." She said she even had a copy of the newsletter in her files and pulled it out while they were on the phone. She said there was one shelter from the list that was still in business in Syracuse. At the time it was called the Men's and Women's Reserve Shelter. She told Ally it was shut down for a while in the early 2000's because of budget cuts. It was post- 9/11 and a lot of charities suffered because of a loss of funding. But then in 2013, an anonymous millionaire created an endowment and the shelter was reestablished for women and children only, and the name was changed to Lexi's House. Today it had a full-time staff and depended on private donations.

Dr. Newton seemed to have a great deal of knowledge about this particular shelter and went on. "It has security cameras and is strictly locked down, and even has security guards on duty at all times. Frankly, no expense is spared. I suspect the benefactor had personal experience with a family member who was abused," surmised Newton. Then she told Ally that she was in regular contact with the shelter, as she continues to help them find volunteers from her classes and also from the nursing program. She said they'd made a huge difference in the community. The original backer had left a trust when he died and they had a very active board as a consequence. They continue to have fundraisers, of course, because there is always such a need.

Ally asked Dr. Newton what she thought the chances were of finding someone who remembered Katie and the family she had helped back in 1991, but didn't expect the response she got.

Dr. Newton replied simply, "I believe your chances are very good."

Chapter - 19

Katie

Since I'd first seen Anna and the children on a Friday, I just set that up as my weekly visit. I wrote to my father and explained to him that I'd taken a part-time job as a babysitter for a wealthy family with four children. They were very active, I told him, and it would be very helpful for me to have a car to get there and back and to transport them to their games and other activities. I asked for $3,000. I told him I'd found a used Chevy Nova in decent condition and thought it would be a good choice. My father, being the kind man that he is, did not ask any questions but sent me a check for $3,000. I hated that I could not tell him the truth, at least not yet.

Now I would have a reliable source of transportation to the shelter and could stay as long as I needed to. On Friday, Oct. 11th, I arrived at the shelter a little before one in the afternoon. I used my new pass key to enter through the front door. The receptionist looked at me with a frightened look on her face. "Has something happened?" I asked, feeling a sense of dread.

Rosie's office door opened suddenly and I could see Anna in there with Caroline. "Quickly Katie, come in here."

"What's going on?" I asked Rosie.

"We've had a breach."

I asked her what that meant and Rosie asked an aide to take Caroline back to their room and to continue watching all three children "very closely."

Once they'd left, Rosie told me that Caroline had gotten turned around and walked out of the facility through a door that automatically locks when closed. She was pretty sure she'd seen one of her father's friends outside.

"So how serious is it at this point? "I asked.

Anna replied. "My husband is a cruel person. He abused me physically and drank too much. He slapped me for no reason just a few days before I came here and left the house. I had no way to contact him. He left me with very little money and I have, as you know, three children to feed and clothe."

I didn't know what to say so I kept quiet as Anna explained how she'd ended up at the shelter. "I had a great job when we were first married. I continued working after I had each of the girls. He worked for the transit authority as a bus driver. We both had good jobs, so we were able to buy a house. We rarely went on vacations but we were happy. A couple of years ago he began drinking. He would stop by the local bar after work instead of coming home and taking care of things that needed to be taken care of. One night when he got home I complained about this and he hit me so hard I fell down. I was stunned. He swore he would never do it again and I forgave him. We vowed to work on our problems and it was going pretty well for a while.

"For the girls' birthdays that year, we decided to take a real vacation and we took them on a Disney Cruise. That's when I got pregnant with Joey. Max was over the moon when we found out it was a boy. We decided I'd resign from my job just before Joey was born and would stay home with the children, which I hadn't done with the girls. Then Max was laid off the following month.

"The abuse started again and became am almost daily thing. Hewould not look for a job and just laid around expecting me to wait on

him. There was another incident of abuse when he put his hands around my neck and bent me back so far I thought my back would break. Then he shoved me to the floor and I had a bad open wound on my elbow and a bruise on my knee. I called the police and they came out and wrote it up and took pictures. They said I would have to be willing to press charges for them to do anything. I did not want to press charges at that time, huh, I bet that is what all the women say the first time?" Rosie just nodded at Anna, like she understood.

"I couldn't keep him happy. If I bought anything that he considered frivolous he would throw it across the room. He expected me to go to Goodwill to buy all the children's clothes and toys. I just couldn't let my babies be brought up with no joy or happiness.

"In the short time we've been here, I've seen such a change in Monica. Her eyes light up every time she sees Katie," Anna said as she smiled at me. "Now I'm afraid he'll find us and will force us to return to the house. I never took out a restraining order so other than the report they wrote up along with the pictures taken, the police have never been involved."

Rosie and I looked at each other, then I said, "I think I can help." Rosie asked what I meant and I said, "I think I can give Anna enough money to get a new start."

"I can't let you do that," said Anna.

"It's the only way for you to stay safe," I said to her. I told them both that I was going to look for a place to rent and that I would pay the first month. "I have the money my father sent me to buy a used car. He thinks I babysit for a family with children. Yes, I lied to him, but I plan to explain everything when I see him this Thanksgiving. I know he'd want me to help you instead."

I assured Anna I would look for a place somewhere her husband would not think to look. "I really want to help keep you and the children safe." Of course, now I realized I wouldn't have a car to drive, so I'd have to see about getting a ride home for Thanksgiving. If I could get to Philly, I could call my brother for a ride home from his fraternity house but, of course, I'd have to let him in on my secret.

Chapter - 20

When I got back to campus, I found a newspaper in the dorm lobby and noticed a few possibilities for rental apartments in the housing ads. The first one I called had already been rented. The second did not answer and the third did not sound very child-friendly. I called another that was described as a 'duplex', though I didn't know what that meant, and a soft voice answered. I had trouble hearing her, but when I told her I was calling about the ad, she perked up and said "Oh yes, it's still available!"

I asked her what 'duplex' meant and she explained that it was a house divided into two units that were mirror images of each other. She owned it and lived in one of the halves. She said it was a two bedroom with a small third bedroom that could be used as an office. "The third room does not have a closet so I can't technically call it a bedroom. It has one bathroom, a nice kitchen and a large family room. There's even a small front porch." She asked me my name, introduced herself as Eleanor Lee, then asked if I wanted to come by to see it. She told me she had just lost a long-time renter who had been attending graduate school, but moved out when he finished. "He was a great tenant and left the place in excellent shape," she assured me. She'd just had it repainted and replaced the carpet. "I think you would really like it. Is it for just yourself?"

She clearly wanted to know if I had a husband or live-in boyfriend or girlfriend. "No, actually I'm calling for a friend who has three young children and is recently widowed," I lied. I made arrangements to see the place the next day, on Saturday. I decided to take a cab because the bus lines change on Saturdays and it would be too hard to figure out the schedule.

Mrs. Lee gave me the address and we settled on a time. She said she had only one other person scheduled to look at it and hadn't had any other calls yet. "I think your friend will love it."

Chapter - 21

Ally

Ally happily returned from the veterinarian's office, where she learned that little Lucky was indeed a boy. He was healthy and was given all the shots that were due a kitten. While there, she purchased recommended kitten food and medication for fleas and worms. She wanted him off to a good start in life. He was tired from the morning excitement so as soon as they were home, he jumped up on her new chair and quickly fell asleep.

There was a voicemail from the coroner's office, which Ally anxiously returned. After confirming that Ally had the approval of the next of kin to be given pertinent information about the remains of Katie Morgan, Dr. Shannon Burns confirmed that, yes, there is more rapid decomposition of bones in salt water but that they had no way of telling how long Katie's body had been in the water. They all believed the body had been protected and possibly snagged next to a shore, somewhere along the coast where it had never been discovered but some weather event probably caused the body to be dislodged and move out into the salt water. Science could not answer all the questions, unfortunately. She said they do the best they can but it just wasn't possible after so long to estimate the time or place she'd been put in the water. At least they were able to identify her, said Dr. Burns. "I pray that brings some closure and maybe comfort to her family."

Ally wanted to pass on to the Morgans what she'd learned and to ask if they would be willing to finance a trip for her go to Syracuse so she could do some deeper investigating. She called Marie to find out if they could see her now.

"Absolutely, darling, come on over."

Marie welcomed her with a hug. She introduced her to Larry. Ally could see the strain on his face. He had probably been thinking more about his lost little girl in the last week than he had in many years. Ally hoped she would be able to find some answers to the long list of questions about Katie's death and leave her parents to finally bury their daughter in peace. She had decided she was fully invested now, and would do anything she could to find out what happened to Katie Morgan.

"First of all," Ally began, "I heard back from the coroner's office, but they said they have no way of knowing when Katie died or how long her body was in the water. The coroner suggested a couple of scenarios, but there's really no way of knowing anything for sure. We have to assume that she was kidnapped and killed, then placed in the sea, either near a bridge or by boat. If she was wrapped securely in a tarp, the bone decomposition would have been slowed immensely, so that's the working theory of law enforcement and the coroner. That much, at least, has been to our benefit, because otherwise there wouldn't have been any bones to be washed up. The coroner said they were relieved to have dental forensics to identify her, so that's something."

The couple looked disappointed but glad that someone was at least pursuing the case, and held hands as Ally went on. "The other things I need to bring you up to date on are more relevant and even promising." Ally told them about her conversation with Dr. Newton, who remembered the solicitation for volunteers all those years ago because she was directly connected to it as a young psychology student.

She said, they'd been overwhelmed with the response and were able to staff several of the organizations for the entire school year. She also had a vague recollection of the disappearance of a nursing student, but it hadn't occurred to her that there might've been a connection with the shelter, not knowing that Katie volunteered there."

Ally waited for all of it to sink in before continuing. "I think if I could just go to Syracuse and visit that shelter, I might be able to track down some clues about Katie's disappearance. I don't think her volunteering and her disappearance are a coincidence, especially after what that letter told us." She paused a moment, feeling a bit uncomfortable at the prospect of asking for money, but she couldn't afford to do this on her own so she knew she had no choice. She took a deep breath and said, "I would need financing, though. At the moment, I'm not able to afford to do this myself, so I'd like to know if you have enough confidence in me that you would finance a trip for me to Syracuse." She just stared at them nervously.

The response was instantaneous. "Of course, we'll finance your trip," replied Marie, and Larry nodded enthusiastically. "Without question," he said firmly. Marie smiled as tears ran down her face. "This is the closest we've come to finding answers. How soon can you go?" she asked.

When she got home, Ally was abuzz with anticipation about her upcoming trip. She was so excited by the prospect of finally making some headway in her little investigation and was even a bit surprised at her own commitment to the case. First she returned Neal's call. He'd left a message saying he'd be coming down that weekend and wanted to see her. She said she had to work on Friday night but could see him on Sunday. They agreed on brunch at one o'clock and he said he'd pick her up.

Then she called Mary to cancel their consignment shopping trip for the time being. "Things have progressed in the Morgan case and I'll be going out of town next week. I just need to get some things done around here."

Mary said she'd be happy to take care of Lucky, which was a relief, since Ally wasn't sure what she'd do with him otherwise.

Chapter - 22

Katie

"I found Cline St without any problem." It was a lovely short street with well-kept homes in an old neighborhood. There were smaller homes and just a couple of duplexes. 677 Cline St was set back from the road and had an old garage in the back that looked like it was not currently being used. Mrs. Lee answered the door after pulling back the side curtain. She invited me in and offered me tea or most any other drink but I said water would be just fine. The weather was turning and I had my North Face jacket on, so had become quite warm and even dehydrated on my walk from the bus stop.

Mrs. Lee took me over to see the other unit. It had a double lock and the new paint smell was still in the air. The place was immaculate. There was even a small oak table in the kitchen with four chairs. "My last renter did not want to keep the table set so he asked if he could just leave it and I said of course!"

I asked about schools.

"Oh yes, there is a very good grammar school just a couple of blocks away," she told me.

I asked about the area, like for shopping and libraries and so on. She said there was a great grocery store just about a mile away, and a library, shopping mall and movie theater nearby as well.

"This area was built to be self-sufficient," she explained, "then the city built out this way and now we have a bus line but very little crime. Our police department is terrific and I think they're pretty responsive, though I haven't had to call for anything," she said.

I liked the idea of a responsive police department, but I hoped Anna would never need it.

Finally, I asked her about the rent and what it included. She said she wanted to make sure the rent was reasonable so she was only asking $550 a month and that included water and sewer. She assured me that the utilities were quite reasonable as well.

I loved the place and thought the location was perfect for Anna. I could see the children being safe and I wanted to help Anna get established. I knew I had to fill Mrs. Lee in on the situation because she might not want to rent to someone fleeing from her spouse.

I looked her in the eye and said, "Mrs. Lee, I have a confession. The woman I'm looking for is not a widow. Everything else is true, but she and her children are actually hiding from her abusive husband and they're currently in a shelter. Something happened yesterday to cause her to be compromised so we have to get them out of there for their safety." All of a sudden, I surprised myself and started sobbing uncontrollably. I hadn't realized how much Anna's situation had been affecting me.

"Oh, my, I'm so sorry, dear. Here you go, "said Mrs. Lee, handing me a box of tissues. "It's OK. You're doing a very good thing." She paused a moment, then said quietly, "My own mother was abused. Not by my father, as he passed away when I was only a year old. But she remarried because it was very difficult financially for a single woman to raise a child back then. It was just after the war and jobs for women were disappearing. So my mother married a man she met at a church social and he turned out to be anything but a Christian man. Luckily, she had enough sense to get out of the situation quickly. One day after he left for work, she packed up all our belongings and we left. She had saved up some money from her grocery budget. She was so smart. Of course I didn't know anything about this until many years later when I was learning how to be a wife." Mrs. Lee smiled at me as she thought of her mother. "She'd saved enough to purchase two train tickets, so we came here with only our clothes from

Youngstown, Ohio. She even laughed about it many years later. She always told me she would have loved to have been a fly on the wall to see his face when he came home that day. She never found out anything else about him. 'Let sleeping dogs lie', she always said. And he was definitely a dog!" she joked.

I finally calmed down. Mrs. Lee got me another glass of water and said, "I'll tell you what I'll do. If you'll make the first month's rent, I'll consider that a deposit and I won't charge your friend rent until she's found a job."

"Really, you would do that?" I asked, shocked at her generosity.

"Yes," she said. "My mother told me that many people in this community reached out to help her when we came here and I want to pay it forward. My mother met a wonderful man later and they even gave me a baby sister. I loved my stepfather very much."

I was so touched by this lovely woman that I couldn't speak for a while. We sat and talked about my being a nursing student.

She said, "That would've been the profession I would've gone into if I hadn't met my dear husband. We had a wonderful forty-five years together until I lost him to cancer. We were not blessed with children but we were happy and he left me without any debt or worries."

When I left, I told Mrs. Lee I would be back with Anna as soon as possible. I also gave her Anna's phone number. She told me to tell Anna not to worry about setting up utilities right now because she would cover them for the time being. I was literally speechless.

I took the bus back to the shelter and told Anna and Rosie all about finding the duplex. I told them about the tremendous generosity of Mrs. Lee. "I think the Good Lord is looking down and taking care of you, Anna."

Anna nodded and said a quiet prayer. "What do we do next?" she asked.

I told her she needed to go to the duplex and see it for herself before making the payment. I filled her in on the grocery store and the grammar school nearby. Rosie said she would help her get some furniture together. Apparently the shelter had a warehouse full of donated furniture for situations just like this. They also had churches they could call on to help move everything. "We could have everything there in a day."

I called Mrs. Lee and arranged for Anna to see the place on Monday morning, and told her she'd bring a check with her. I told Anna I wouldn't be able to go with her because I had classes on Monday so she should take a cab there and back. We all agreed it was too risky for her to be out in public taking a bus.

Rosie even said they had a cab company that offers free rides to people from the shelter as a community service. She was also going to contact the church to arrange for a quick move. Anna was overwhelmed and could not believe all the help she was getting. I was so relieved that it was all coming together!

Chapter - 23

Ally

Since Ally had a work function on Friday night, she told the Morgans she wouldn't be able to fly out of town until Monday. She had arranged to meet with Dr. Newton when she arrived, who would then take her to the shelter and introduce her around. Having Dr. Newton vouch for her would make it much easier for Ally to find answers to her questions without raising suspicions.

She arrived at the clubhouse at six o'clock on Friday night as instructed. She met the bartender, Regina, who told Ally the crowd was older and typically only have one or two cocktails each. The women mostly drank wine so she had two generic white wines and two reds queued up.

Ally walked around to the back and saw Gene, looking as handsome as ever. He came up to her and said, "I hate to tell you this now but the other server called out." He said he was very sorry but he wasn't able to get anyone else. "I'll do my best to help you but I'll mostly be handling things in the catering truck. This clubhouse doesn't have a kitchen so everything has to be done out of here."

"Okay," nodded Ally apprehensively. "But I have to tell you something too," she added.

Gene looked at her nervously, seeming certain she was about to quit on him.

"No, no, don't worry. It's just that I'm flying to New York on Monday for about a week, maybe less, so I won't be available for the next week."

Gene looked relieved and thanked her for letting him know. "Do you need your paycheck before you go?" he surprised her by asking.

"Oh, that would be great!"

He told her he would have it ready by Monday morning if she wanted to swing by and pick it up.

"That would be perfect. I'm flying out of Wilmington so I'll stop by on my way to the airport. Thank you for thinking of it."

The evening was uneventful. The honored guest loved everything and thanked his wife for the party and his friends for coming. They turned on some music via an Alexa they had hooked up and everyone started dancing to 60's music. The party started to thin out around nine-thirty. Everyone looked tired but seemed to have enjoyed themselves. They were very complimentary of the food, which pleased Gene. Ally helped with the clean-up and loading the truck and they were out of there by eleven.

On Saturday, Ally caught up on chores and then went to the local nail salon for a much-needed mani and pedi. She spent the rest of the afternoon packing and paying bills before turning in early. She needed a good night's sleep because she knew she had a long week ahead.

The next morning, Neal picked her up and they went to a popular favorite brunch place in Calabash. It was nothing fancy but they made Ally's favorite dish: shrimp and grits. Neal could sense she was tense and finally asked her why she was so quiet. Ally decided to tell him the whole story of Katie Morgan. She had mentioned it to him once before but had not told him of her involvement. She said she'd be gone a few days, maybe three, starting Monday. She said she was more worried about *not* finding anything than finding something that would help solve the mystery of Katie's murder.

"No one has any idea why Katie just disappeared. I'm hoping this shelter will finally lead to some useful clues."

Neal listened intently. "Ally, this could be dangerous, I hope you know that."

"Oh, I suppose, maybe." She hadn't really thought about her own safety. "But it's been so many years, Neal, I can't imagine there's anyone out there who would be looking to harm me for asking questions."

Neal said, "You know my name is Smith, a common name. Well, Ally, my mother's name was Louisa Costa. Her grandparents changed their surname to Cotton when they emigrated from Italy. There were dangerous people in Sicily who her grandfather had angered, and family feuds never died there. I'm not trying to scare you, I'm just trying to say that danger tends to lurk wherever seedy characters abound."

"Okaaaay," Ally said. "But I'm pretty determined to get to the truth," she assured him.

"I know, just be careful, okay?" Neal warned. "I want you back in one piece," he winked.

The following afternoon, Ally was on a two-thirty flight out of Wilmington. She had a layover at JFK in New York City, but then caught a short commuter flight into Syracuse Hancock International Airport. She finally got in at six forty-five pm and had the evening to collect herself and prepare for the week ahead. She took a taxi to the Holiday Inn Express. She had reservations only for three nights and hoped it would not take longer than that. In the cab on the way to the hotel, she noticed she had a message from Marie Morgan, making sure she'd arrived safely. *Once a mother, always a mother,* Ally thought sadly. She made a mental note to call her in the morning when she was not so tired.

She had arranged to meet Dr. Newton on Tuesday morning at 9:00 am in her office at SU. She was a little nervous about going back to her alma mater. It was hard to believe she hadn't been there in 30 years.

The school had grown so much since Ally had been a student there. She'd kept up her alumni dues and tried reading each alumni magazine that came out. She naturally navigated to the nursing alumni pages. She was proud of her school and the reputation it still maintained. She would recommend it to anyone who asked. Her parents had scrupulously saved to send all their children to college. She could have applied for an academic scholarship but her parents told her there was no need and to let someone who really needed a scholarship have a chance at it. She knew she was lucky to have parents who'd planned for the future. She knew that today's students really struggled to pay the out-of-control tuition at most schools, and was glad that when she was a student it was not nearly as bad. She never forgot how lucky she was to be able to attend Syracuse without the restrictions of a scholarship. She hoped she'd made her parents and her profession proud.

Chapter - 24

The next morning, Ally arrived early. She had slept restlessly with so much on her mind. She had no idea what or how much she would find out and briefly wondered if she really wanted to know the unknown. But she was here now, so she decided to get on with the job at hand. After a standard hotel breakfast, she grabbed a cab outside the hotel and headed to Syracuse University, to the building where Dr. Isabella Newton had her office. After consulting the lobby directory, she made her way to the 5th floor.

Dr. Newton was very warm and inviting. She asked Ally about her flight and if she'd had a restful night.

"I'm afraid I never sleep well away from home," responded Ally.

Dr. Newton laughed and agreed. She offered Ally coffee or tea but Ally declined both.

Dr. Newton told Ally she had scheduled an appointment at ten forty-five at the shelter. In the meantime, she had pulled up some newspaper clippings from the archives regarding the missing nursing student. Ally read through all of them but found no new leads and the police had only said the case was still under investigation. She was sure Marie had the same clippings stored away. That reminded her to give Marie a call. She excused herself so she could step outside and call Marie.

"Well, hello there," Marie answered when she saw Ally's number come up.

"I'm sorry I'm just now calling you but I got in a bit late last night and by the time I got to my hotel I was in the bag. I'm at Dr. Newton's office right now but we have a ten forty-five appointment at the shelter, so we'll be leaving soon to go over there." She promised to call Marie as soon as she had any information.

When she returned to the office, Dr. Newton said, "I think we should leave. You never know about traffic around here."

As they waited for the elevator, Ally asked, "How long have you been a professor?"

"Not that long, really. I went into private practice once I finished graduate school. I had student loans to pay back and thought that would be the fastest way to do it. After I had them mostly paid off, a position came open for an Associate Professor of Psychology, so I applied. After two years, there was a death on the faculty and I became a full professor. I hate to say it but I was lucky that someone died, because it doesn't usually happen that quickly," she smirked. "I'll be up for tenure in two more years. So, I'm more or less pledged to Syracuse for the rest of my career. The only thing I do not like is the weather. I'm a southern California girl at heart," she smiled.

They reached the garage and Dr. Newton's car. It was a Subaru Forester. Dark green with tan interior, leather seats. *Very nice,* noted Ally.

It was a forty-five minute drive to the shelter and they arrived a little early. Dr. Newton used her own pass card to enter the facility. The receptionist knew her and led them into a small conference room with a TV screen mounted on the far wall. It also had a side table holding pamphlets about the facility. Ally looked over them. It was all very impressive.

A woman entered and introduced herself as Cecelia Bond. "I'm the Director of Admissions. I'll be glad to help you if I can. Dr. Newton brought me up to date on your request and I've gone back through our records but could only find one possibility that might help you. Based on the dates and on the reports of the young woman who went missing, we could only find one family that matches." She pulled out a file and set it infront of her on the table before continuing. "The previous director, Rosie McMahon, kept immaculate records. Unfortunately, they're thirty years old and some were damaged or lost when we remodeled, so the folders did not all stay together. But there is hope. Rosie is still alive, although she is in a rest home. But she's still pretty sharp and I think she would be your best bet to get more information. As it's such a long time ago and she no longer works here, she wouldn't be held to any confidentiality clause." She paused and looked at Ally sympathetically. "I'd like to help this poor girl's family, but this is the best information we have at this time. The last name of the family was Strickland. The mother was Anna."

Ally felt a sudden swell of relief that her journey had not been wasted and that she now had a real lead. She let out a grateful sigh and said, "I can't tell you how much I appreciate this. I think this will be very helpful."

"I'm very glad to hear that. I wish you the best of luck," said Cecelia sincerely. She gave Ally the address of the rest home and a business card with a short note on the back to give to the director as an introduction. "I'll call ahead so Rosie will be expecting you." Ally thanked her profusely and almost hugged her as she and Dr. Newton left.

Unfortunately, Dr. Newton had a class at two forty-five that she could not miss, so after they'd enjoyed a nice lunch together, she suggested Ally get an Uber or cab to the rest home if she wanted to go that afternoon.

Ally thanked Dr. Newton for all her help and for arranging everything for her. "I don't have the words to express my gratitude," she said with tears in her eyes. Dr. Newton told her she was glad to help and to please let her know the outcome, whether good or bad. Ally promised she would.

Ally hailed a cab and sat in the back seat quietly contemplating how she would react when she met the person who might hold the clue to how Katie Morgan had died. She was about to find out about the woman who had sent Katie that letter that had been missing for so many years. Her heart was pounding. When they pulled up to the Shady Grove Rest Home, Ally paid the fare and walked into the facility, proceeding to the reception desk.

Ally explained why she was there and who she wanted to visit. The receptionist asked her to sign in and called for an attendant to show her to Rosie. She was escorted to a patio off the side of the building. It was covered with a pergola and was very well maintained. A woman with curly gray hair was sitting in a wheelchair with a book in her lap and looking absently out over the lawn. She turned toward Ally as the attendant gestured toward her and then left, and Ally knew she had found Rosie.

Ally handed Rosie the card from Cecelia Bond and introduced herself.

"I knew one day someone would come with the questions you're about to ask me," said Rosie, nodding sadly.

Chapter - 25

Anna

Anna got a cab just as Rosie had instructed and was not charged a fare She arrived on Cline St. and before she exited the cab she was already in love with the place. She thanked the driver and nervously made her way to the door. Before she got to the door Katie had told her to go to, a woman came out and opened her arms. "I am so glad to see you, Anna," greeted Mrs. Lee. "Please come in for some tea or coffee so we can chat." Anna knew this was going to be the place for her.

Mrs. Lee had some cinnamon buns set out along with a fruit bowl of bananas, blueberries and strawberries. Since Anna had been too nervous to eat that morning, it was a welcome treat. They had coffee, black, and enjoyed the simple breakfast. Mrs. Lee asked Anna about her children. Anna proudly told her about all three. She said Joey was just about to crawl and she worried about stairs and other dangers. Mrs. Lee assured her there were no stairs in the duplex and he would not be able to get out the doors.

"There's only the front door, which has two locks and a back door with a screen that can be latched." She started describing the duplex but then said, "Why don't we just go over there so you can see your new home for yourself?"

Anna was so happy as they toured the unit. It was immaculate, with fresh paint and new carpet. She could not believe Katie had found such a wonderful safe haven for her and the children. Anna told Mrs. Lee how impressed she was with the house.

She gave her Katie's check for $550. "I cannot thank you enough for your generosity. I know I'll be able to find a job soon. I used to work in an insurance office and think I can brush up on my skills." She promised to start looking right away.

"I don't suppose you know of a reasonable daycare center around here?" she asked tentatively, knowing the older, childless woman probably had no connections to any daycare.

"As a matter of fact, I do," said Mrs. Lee, nodding.

"Really? That's a relief. I'll need to call and enroll the girls quickly," Anna said.

"You won't need to enroll them, Anna. I will be happy to take care of your children," said Mrs. Lee with a kind smile. Then she added, "Unless you don't want me to, of course. I guess I am being presumptuous."

Anna did not know what to say. She stuttered "You-you would do that for me?"

"Of course, dear, it would be my pleasure and my joy. You would actually be doing me a favor. My greatest regret is not having children. My sister had three girls but my husband and I never had any of our own. Yours will be like my grandchildren... I mean, unless they already have grandparents in their life?"

"No," said Anna, "my parents were killed in a car accident when I was eighteen. I think that's why I married so young. I do have a brother but he left home after they were killed and I don't hear from him very much." Anna was lying to her, and felt guilty about it, and knew she would have to contact her mother at some point, but she would confess to Mrs. Lee when the time came. It was just too much for her to think about at the moment.

"If you're absolutely sure, it would be an honor to have you watch over my children while I work, but I'll pay you as soon as I'm in a position

to do so."

Mrs. Lee assured her that it would all work out in time.

Two days later a large moving truck pulled up in front of Mrs. Lee's house with all the furniture the Strickland family would need. The movers were volunteers and they even refused a tip. Anna promised herself that once she got in a better financial position, she would help the charities that had helped her and pay it forward.

By the end of the week, she had enrolled Caroline in school and had listed only herself and Mrs. Lee as the two people who would be allowed to sign her out of school.

The following Monday, Anna started earnestly looking for a job. She found an accounting office a few blocks away that was owned by a woman who preferred hiring women. Unusual concept, Anna thought, but it sure sounded good to her. She had to take a drug test and, of course, passed it. Then she was given a typing test and passed with flying colors. She was hesitant to give her previous employment information, although she knew they would want to check her references. She finally broke down and told the owner about her situation and that she was trying to make a clean break from her abusive husband. She told her she had called the police one time, which was true, but she did not follow through with filing charges. They kept the record and had pictures of her wounds and bruises, in case more came of it, I guess. I never got to the phase of a legal separation, although, that is where I am heading, I'm sure. The owner felt sorry for her and told her she would help her find a pro bono attorney to help her file for a legal separation. The woman said she would hire Anna if she promised to follow through and if a divorce is what she plans to do she will help her with that too. Anna asked her why she would help her so much. The woman said, I've been there and I was helped. I am simply paying it forward.

A few weeks went by after they got moved in and Anna admitted to Mrs. Lee that she had a mother and siblings that lived in Danville and she could have gone to them, but at the time she was not thinking straight and knew her mother did not have enough room for all of them. Besides, isn't that the first place my husband would look for us? Mrs. Lee comforted her and told her it was okay but that it was time she made it right with *her mother. So that evening she called her mother and she spilled her guts about everything that had happened. Her mother was unusually patient with her. Anna knew she had experienced some domestic violence when her father was alive, but she would never speak of it. She wondered if it was possible for a woman to escape it. She assured her mother that the children were well and she had a lovely lady who was her neighbor in the duplex and her landlord and how generous she had been. She explained she had given her a very reasonable rent amount and was including utilities in it. "I had a most unlikely but blessed experience while I was at the shelter. A volunteer student there wanted so badly to help that she gave me $3,000 to help us get started and she wanted nothing in return.. It is too bad that I won't ever see her again."*

Mrs. Turner said, "Anna, I know it will be hard but I think you need to swallow your pride and let Max know that you and the children are ok. I know it will take every ounce of pride and energy you have to do this but you truly owe the father of you children an explanation. Do you agree?"

"I have been praying about it, mom, and you are right as usual. I just have to get up my nerve."

"Well, good. Would it be okay for me to come see you next month? I need your address and telephone number." Anna readily agreed and gave her mother what she requested.

Later that evening, after getting the girls in the bed and doing prayers with them and getting baby Joey in his crib in her room, she kneeled on the floor and asked God to forgive her and asked for the courage it will take her to contact Max, but she knows she must do this.

Chapter - 26

Ally and Rosie

Rosie McMahon gazed off into the distance for a moment, as if she was in a trance, but quickly snapped out of it and looked directly at Ally. "I always had a gut feeling that Katie Morgan's disappearance had something to do with her helping a particular family in our shelter. "But I couldn't say anything to the police because I worried it could have jeopardized the family's safety."

She told Ally about how Katie had become attached to a family of four that had arrived at the shelter shortly after she started volunteering. "One of the little girls had gotten turned around and gone outside, where she thought she'd seen a friend of her father's, so we were all worried that he would tell her father where he had seen her. The father was a driver for some company - Walmart, maybe. At the time, his wife said he was out on a run that would last about two weeks, so we basically had about a week left before he returned and found out his wife had left and taken the children. Anna – that was the mother's name - was desperate to get the children and herself away from him. When Katie found out they were in danger, she jumped into action. She found them a place to live and used money her father had given her for a car to pay the first month's rent."

Rosie sighed heavily before continuing. "She knew the money wouldn't go very far but everyone expected Anna would be able to find a job and receive some financial help from the state so she could stay clear of her abusive husband. Katie found an apartment almost right away. Within days, Anna and her children were moved in and everything had worked out. I do remember telling Katie, though, that for the family's safety, she would not be able to see them again, but that we'd be pleased to have her continue as one of our valued volunteers. She came every Thursday and Friday afternoon right up until she went missing."

"So what happened to the family? Did they hear about what happened to Katie?" asked Ally.

Rosie couldn't say for sure, since they'd cut off contact once they'd moved, but she suspected Anna was too afraid of going to the police because she worried her husband might find out where she was. And there was never any evidence that he had anything to do with Katie's disappearance, after all.

"So, Katie goes missing, the police have no suspects or clues as to what happened to her and everyone goes on about their business?" Ally realized she sounded angry.

Rosie looked at Ally with tears in her eyes and said, "As ashamed as I am now about it, I'm afraid that's true. Believe me when I say everyone at the shelter was sad and depressed. We cried with her family every time we saw them on TV. Please remember we would have had no idea if the father even knew Katie or if he could have linked her to his missing family."

Ally thanked Rosie for her honesty and apologized if her visit had caused her distress. The two women hugged and Rosie wished her success in her search, asking Ally to please let her know if she ever finds out what happened to Katie.

Chapter - 27

Ally

Ally was scheduled to fly home the next morning, but first she went back to SU. She visited the nursing school and spoke with the Dean. She was very impressed with how the campus had grown since she'd been a student. She located Dr. Newton in her office and shared what she'd learned from Rosie. "It's disappointing to have come this far and still have nothing to tell the Morgans about how their daughter died."

"That may be," replied Dr. Newton, "but you can tell them how she lived – how much she cared for those people and what a good and decent young woman she was. I think that's probably even more important than how she died, don't you? They'll be very proud of her dedication and sacrifice."

Dr. Newton reassured Ally that she was doing all she could do. "At least they have her remains and can finally give her a proper burial," she reassured Ally.

"That's true," nodded Ally. She thanked Dr. Newton for her help and said she'd let her know if she turned up any new information or found the Stricklands, and they bid farewell.

Ally turned her car in at the airport rental terminal and headed to the gate. She had an easy flight into JFK and the second leg of the flight went well. Her seatmate was a distinguished looking gentleman. He introduced himself to her and asked if she had been visiting or was headed south to visit. She told him she was headed south where she now lived and was proud of it. He asked how she liked the area she lived and she let him know it was paradise compared to the cold northeast.

"No more snow shovels for me," she added.

He chuckled and said, "I agree, it would be wonderful to get out of that for a change."

She asked out of curiosity what he did for a living.

"FBI," he told her without elaborating. She figured he thought if you just said FBI, that would explain everything.

"Well, Mr. Langford, I have a few questions for you if you are willing. I understand if it is not your area of expertise."

"Okay, what would you like to ask me?"

"For starters, do you handle murder cases, especially ones that are thirty years old?"

"No, that is not my area of expertise, but tell me what you know and I will see if I can get you help."

Ally spent the next half hour telling Mr. Langford about the skeletal remains and how she knew her from college and remembered when she went missing. "Now we have a name of Anna Strickland, that we have been told was the last person Katie was associated with and we have no idea how to find her. She was at a Shelter in Syracuse and Katie helped her get out and found a home for her and her three children. It was a brave thing to do. She disappeared about three weeks later."

"Coincidence?"

"They don't know. Without finding this Anna Strickland, I don't have any further information on how their path ended."

"If I were you, I would contact the driver's license bureau and see if there is a license in her name and if there are any, you know, citations or arrests. If she is clean, it may be a little harder. Strickland is not a real common name but on the other hand she could have changed her name or just started using her maiden name. Go back aways in your search, you might get lucky and connect her to another license. Also, check voter registration rolls. They don't clean them up enough and you may find her there."

Ally had not thought of any of this. She thanked Mr. Langford and he wished her well in her pursuits.

By this time the pilot came on and said they were about to land in Wilmington.

Ally was so happy to see Lucky when she got home, she hugged and kissed him until he squirmed and jumped out of her arms. Mary had come in each day and fed and played with him, so Ally was relieved he hadn't been lonely. She called Three Island Catering and spoke with Sara. She asked if there was any work for her that weekend and Sara said, "There sure is, we need you!"

Apparently, they had booked two wedding receptions on Saturday, one in the afternoon and another in the evening. She was glad to hear that she would definitely be needed. Next she called Mary and asked her to come down for a glass of wine. When she arrived, Ally gave her a beautiful pillow she had bought at the airport gift shop as a Thank You for taking care of Lucky. It said "There is nothing a man can do that a woman can't do better."

Mary loved it and then said, "I think I'm going to start dating again. You inspired me to think about it. I never thought it would be right for me but I've changed my mind." Ally was pleased to hear she'd had a positive effect on her friend.

The next day Ally called Marie to discuss her trip and Marie told her to come for lunch around one o'clock. When Marie opened the door, Ally handed her a beautiful bouquet of flowers. Marie looked surprised. "Oh, my! What's the occasion?" she asked.

Ally told her that she just felt like giving Marie and Larry flowers because they were her friends. They all sat down to lunch on the back deck, where they could enjoy the sunshine.

Ally paused and cleared her throat, then said, "I've gotten to know both of you because of the worst experience any parents could ever have. And even though I don't have the answer to how Katie died or who killed her - at least not yet - I can tell you what she was doing just before she disappeared, and I know you'll be proud."

Ally told them about the volunteer job Katie had taken on almost the first week of school, and about the family she had encountered who were hiding from an abusive husband and father. She couldn't offer many details but she felt like she knew enough to say, "Suffice it to say, your daughter saw a need and acted on it. She performed a true measure of kindness."

She told them about Katie using the $3,000 they given her for a car to help this family and that she'd found them a safe place to live out of the shelter. "She continued to volunteer at the shelter until she went missing, but that's all I have for you right now."

Ally explained that the shelter hadn't contacted the police because they worried it could expose the family and they had no proof that the father had anything to do with Katie's disappearance. She also explained that the retired director of the shelter to whom she'd spoken had presumed that the woman Katie had helped escape her husband had not gone to the police for the same reasons.

"I do have a name of the woman Katie helped. It is Anna Strickland. It makes sense since the letter was signed by Anna. My seat mate on the flight home was an FBI agent and he gave me some helpful information on how to perhaps locate this Anna. I will start the search as soon as I can. I hope that helps you some."

Marie cried as Larry comforted her. Ally sat in silence, trying not to become emotional herself.

Larry finally said, "We're having a service for Katie at the cemetery where her grandparents are buried. The coroner released her remains to us, so she's being cremated and the ashes will be kept by our sons and spread on our graves after we're both gone. It'll be on November 9th, the day she went missing. We hope you'll attend."

Ally thanked him and said she would be honored to be there.

Part - 2

———•———

Chapter - 28

Three months later

Ally had returned last night from visiting her parents in Florida and had decided to catch up on her emails. It is now February and a little chilly outside. She had enjoyed the warm Florida sunshine for too long. She'd only been gone for a few days but it had been a road trip and she was exhausted from the drive. About halfway through her emails she came upon one from Marie. All it said was for Ally to please contact her when she could. Ally had not spoken with Marie since Christmas. She hoped nothing had happened to Larry.

She immediately called and when Marie answered she said, "Oh Ally, I'm so glad to hear from you; you won't believe what happened!"

Marie said she'd received a call from a producer for the show Real Mysteries. They said they wanted to do a feature on Katie's disappearance and the finding of her remains. The show contacted me and Larry to see if we would be a part of it. Apparently ever since Katie's remains were found they have been doing research on the case and think it would make a compelling show. We would like you to be involved if you are willing. Of course, they know nothing about your efforts to locate Katie's roommates or that you found the shelter where she volunteered. We haven't told them about any of that yet. We were worried you didn't want to be involved or give the shelter any unwanted publicity. But they said after they'd put out feelers in the Syracuse area looking for anyone who might know anything, they were contacted by a woman who said she might have some knowledge about Katie. Her name is Monica Strickland Christopher.

Ally said,, "I tried in vain to locate an Anna Strickland, remember I told you at Christmas, I had no luck. I tried through the DMV but they shut me down. Unless I was with the police or a higher up authority, they do not verify records. We would have had to hire a private eye. I tried the voting rolls but without an address, I could not match anything up. There are more Stricklands in Syracuse than you can imagine but there were no Anna's. I gave up thinking she probably never registered to vote. Some people don't just to stay under the radar or to get out of jury duty. I am glad someone has come forward. Who is she?"

Apparently," Marie said quietly, "when Monica was very young, her mother took her and her sister Caroline and baby brother Joey to a shelter in Syracuse. Monica was too young to realize what was happening but she remembered a girl named Katie used to come every week to play with them and help them with their reading. They all loved her. Then she said they had to move out of the shelter suddenly because some people thought their father might find them, so they moved to a house across town. Her mother got a job and their landlord, Mrs. Lee, would take Caroline to school and pick her up every day. She did the same for Monica and Joey when they were old enough for school. Their mother did make a reconciliation with their father shortly after they moved and he was a part of their lives, getting them on weekends and during the summer. They did officially separate and eventually divorced. The husband, Max, was a long distance truck driver. He remarried and had a child whom they all grew up with. The thing was the little girl was only a few months younger than his son with Anna."

Ally just raised her eyebrows like she understood Marie's meaning. As Marie recounted Monica's story, Ally realized it aligned closely with everything she had discovered. Marie took a breath and continued, "she said Mrs. Lee passed away about 18 years ago and left the house to her mother, mortgage-free, and even left a trust for each of the children. Monica now lives in Mrs. Lee's side of the duplex with her husband and daughter and her mother still lives in the other half, where they all grew up. Her sister, Caroline, moved to Pittsburgh when she got married and

Joey joined the Air Force when he graduated high school. He's now a Major. Apparently Monica wanted Katie's family to know that they are all doing well. They always remembered Katie for her kindness but were told they couldn't see her again for their own safety. They knew almost nothing about her except that she was a nursing student from Syracuse University."

"Wow, that's all amazing, Marie. So what now?" asked Ally, feeling surprisingly hopeful about the situation.

"Larry and I want to meet Monica and her family but we want you to come with us. That's why we waited for you to get back from your trip to Florida."

"Oh, Marie, I would love to be there," said Ally gratefully. She thought after meeting with Dr. Newton and talking with Rosie that her participation had ended, but she knew it was important to Marie that she be a part of Katie's continuing story. "Just give me some notice when you're scheduling the meeting so I can be available, in case there are catering jobs I'm needed on, okay?"

Marie told Ally she'd talk to the producer and see how they wanted to handle it.

When they hung up, Ally checked in at work and Sara said they could use her that evening. "Gene's best friend was killed in a car accident so he's on a plane on his way to the funeral tomorrow. He thought you might be able to run the event tonight."

"Oh, no, I'm so sorry to hear that, Sara!" exclaimed Ally. "Is he coping alright, I hope? Of course I'll help, anyway I can."

"He's handling it. He's worried about being gone, though. This is a birthday party, a fiftieth. The client is throwing it for his wife at their home. It'll be around twenty-five people and the food are primarily shrimp and grits and ribs. All the food will be ready and Gene arranged to have Jim and Sherry there to help you prepare."

Ally knew that Jim and Sherry, a married couple, had helped Gene on numerous occasions and were very familiar with the business. "Okay, I think I can manage. Please text me the address and time, and pass on my sympathies to Gene if you speak with him."

"You got it. Thanks, Ally," said Sara, sounding relieved.

The party was in three hours and Ally had a lot to do to be ready. Fortunately, she had just washed clothes that morning so her outfit was ready but had to be ironed. She took a shower and fed Lucky, then called Mary to let her know she would be out tonight. They'd started letting each other know if they would be away for any time, especially at night, just for safety's sake.

Ally arrived at the home on Oak Island at five-thirty. The guests were expected around seven. The client had set up tables on the back deck as well as a few inside. She introduced herself and told the couple that they could speak with her about any problems they saw or changes they wanted to make.

The catering truck pulled up at six o'clock. Jim came in to see where the client wanted to set up the buffet. By six-forty-five, everything was presentable. The guests began arriving and Ally settled down a bit. She remained primarily in the kitchen because thankfully there was no serving to be done. She just had to make sure there was enough food out at all times.

The party was in full swing. Music was playing from the Echo Dot set to '60's music. Ally was thinking about the upcoming meeting with Monica Strickland when all of a sudden someone shouted "Help!" She ran out on the deck and found a woman sitting at a table with her hands at her throat; a sure sign of choking. People were just staring at her and looking panicked. Ally ran to the woman, who by this time was pale and in obvious distress. Ally put her nurse hat on and told the man next to her to help stand the woman up and move her chair so she could get behind her. Ally, being about five foot six was a good bit taller than the woman which was an advantage.

With all of her strength, Ally performed the Heimlich maneuver on the woman while nervous guests watched with amazement. It took her two upward motions but the woman spit out a piece of carrot that apparently had not been chewed up well enough. As soon as it was released, she went limp in Ally's arms and with the help of her companion, they sat her back in her chair. She coughed a few more times but then her coloring came back and she seemed shaky, so Ally asked the host if there was a place they could take her to revive herself. The host, a burly man who was clearly unnerved told her of course, and helped Ally take the woman, who could walk with help to a guest bedroom and they had her lay down on the bed with a few pillows propped behind her head. Ally went and got her some water and set it at the bedside. The woman's husband came in the room and thanked Ally for doing what she did. Ally laughed, "All in a day's work. I used to be an RN." The man just looked at her in surprise and said, "Well, Marsha, this is our lucky day as he glanced at his wife." She had a small smile on her face and managed to say "thank you." When Ally went back out to check on the guests, everyone started clapping.

Ally quietly slipped back into her station in the kitchen. Then she almost collapsed. She saw a bottle of Yuengling nearby and grabbed it and opened it before anyone could come in. She took a long swig of the cold beer and felt immediate relaxation. She dumped it down the sink and put the bottle in the recycling. She had a mint in her pocket and popped it into her mouth. Whew, that was a close one! she thought with a huge sigh of relief.

Since it was a small party, Gene hadn't sent in his usual crew, so Ally helped Jim and Sherry with clean up. It only took them about an hour to load up the truck. The shrimp and grits were a huge hit and the ribs were almost all eaten. They packaged them up and left them with the client.

When Ally got home, she called Mary to check in and told her about the choking incident. "I was so glad the woman was small and I could get my arms around her!" she exclaimed. "Otherwise, it might not have turned out so well. I almost had them call the EMS but when I saw her, I thought I'd be able to handle it. It actually felt good to knock off the cobwebs and use some of my nursing skills. The clients and their guests seemed grateful."

Mary's eyes widened as she listened to Ally recap the emergency. When she'd finished, Mary said, "Geez, Ally, I sure hope you're around when I need you!"

They shared a much-needed laugh.

Chapter - 29

Ally had been seeing Neal for almost a year, but only when he came down for weekends, so it was sporadic. This weekend he invited her to his place for dinner and she was looking forward to spending the evening relaxing. Because they lived in a destination place for weddings, the catering business was very competitive, so work had been hectic lately. Luckily things were beginning to settle down. Ally had been promoted to handling the scheduling and Sara had become office manager, and helped Gene with advertising. She'd also taken online courses in sales and management skills. Ally thought they were paying off because the business had seemed busier than when she started with them. But things were beginning to settle down a bit for the season, so Ally was happy to have more time for pleasure.

She arrived at Neal's at seven o'clock wearing a black high-neck backless sundress with her best black slides. She'd been letting her hair grow longer, so she could wear it in a chignon. She wore silver dangling earrings she'd bought at one of the weekend markets held in a nearby town on Saturday mornings. She felt she looked elegant, maybe even a little too elegant for a casual night in.

Neal looked very handsome in his loose white Untuck it shirt and black pants. They looked ready for one of those pictures that are popular on the beach, usually with the dunes in the background. Ally has seen countless family pictures taken like that in the homes of the catering business clients.

Ally brought a chardonnay and a chianti and had made a chopped salad with a homemade vinaigrette. "Uhm, smells wonderful in here," she complimented Neal. He had a vanilla candle lit and then she noticed the red snapper wrapped in cellophane. "Is there anything I can help you with?" she asked.

He said no, gave her a kiss, and told her she looked lovely.

"I hope you haven't gone to too much trouble, Neal," she smiled.

"You'd better hope I have," he said as he winked at her.

She thought this might be the night they became intimate. They had a tremendous sexual attraction to each other and it built every time they were together. She was not the marrying type, so that was not important to her, but if she ever did want to settle down, sex would be the most important thing to make sure the relationship was right. A wise woman had once told her what it takes to be a good wife: "Always be a lady, except in the bedroom, where it doesn't count." Ally had never forgotten that fairly risqué bit of advice.

After a delicious dinner of grilled red snapper and red potatoes cooked to perfection with a little garlic butter, Ally felt great. The wine did not hurt either. They sat on the back deck overlooking the beach. It was a clear night and stars were visible. Ally could hear the rhythmic pounding of the waves as they came in on the beach. It must be high tide, she thought. She was getting use to the sounds of living near the ocean. Neal had his arm around her as they sat on his porch swing.

"Oh, guess what? I had a scare at my last catering job. A guest started choking and I had to give her the Heimlich."

"Wow, I bet you didn't expect your nursing skills to come in handy on a catering job, huh?" asked Neal with surprise.

"Very true," agreed Ally. "I was glad I could help. Everyone else seemed to just freeze and not know what to do."

"Good for you. You just saved a life." He noticed she seemed a littlechilled from the sea breeze so he pulled her to him and soon they began kissing. Things progressed fairly quickly from there, especially since they were both so eager.

She awakened the next morning beside Neal. "Wow, what a night," Ally exhaled.

"Isn't that the start of a Frankie Valli song?" quipped Neal.

"Pretty close, I think," Ally laughed. She knew they had both seen the musical Jersey Boys, about Frankie Valli and the Four Seasons.

"How are you feeling?" asked Neal.

"Couldn't be better," smiled Ally.

"Did you leave enough food out for Lucky last night?" Ally was happy that he'd thought about her darling cat and assured him Lucky had plenty of food and water.

"Let's get coffee and have it out on the porch."

"Great idea," she said, and sat up to look for her underwear and bra, which were on the floor beside the bed, where Neal had helped her remove them. He had jumped up and gone to his closet to toss her one of his shirts. "Boyfriend shirt," she smirked, feeling like a teenager. Neal laughed.

Chapter - 30

Marie called Ally the following Thursday and said the Real Mysteries producer wanted to meet with them and that she'd like Ally to join them, so she was wondering about Ally's schedule for next week. Ally told her she'd check in with work and get back to her as soon as she could. She called work and told Sara she might need some time off the following week. Luckily there was nothing on the books between a wedding this Saturday and another one next Saturday, so her schedule was wide open during the week. She called Marie back and Marie said she'd speak with the producer and get back to Ally with a day and time.

Ally called Mary to tell her she may not make the gym on Monday and wasn't sure about their other days because of this meeting with a producer from Real Mysteries. She was excited but apprehensive about meeting with Monica Christopher. She was more worried about how Marie would hold up. She was so fragile but determined to find out the truth about what happened to Katie. Mary reassured her in her usual calm way.

Then Ally called Neal to fill him in.

"That's great, Ally. Your private detective work is finally paying off, huh?" he joked. "Maybe you'll all find out something that could bring this case to a close."

"Maybe, but it sure is nerve-wracking. I just hope Marie and Larry can find some closure."

"I do too, sweetheart," he said, suddenly melting her heart, which she had not thought could be melted. *Am I falling in love with this man?* she wondered. It was so complicated falling for a man at her age, especially a physician who was established and prosperous in his own right. She had her own money and could live on her own. Why was she so reluctant to make a commitment? She decided not to think about any of that until this Katie Morgan saga was put to rest. At least she knew he was on her side; she was just unsure of his true feelings, or her own, for that matter.

The meeting with Real Mysteries was set for the following Tuesday at the Morgan's home. The producer had also spoken with all four Stricklands, and except for Joey, who was stationed at Ft Hood, Texas and couldn't leave the base, they were all happy to meet with the Morgans whenever it was convenient.

Ally worked the wedding reception on Saturday, but was looking forward to seeing Neal afterwards. He would drive down on Saturday instead of Friday, since she would be busy until later in the evening.

"Just don't be too tired," she teased him flirtatiously.

The wedding reception was held at one of the golf course clubhouses. It was a very lovely setting with beautiful decorations and tiny white lights strung everywhere. The menu was mostly barbeque. Apparently, the groom was a barbecue lover and his new bride decided to surprise him and change the original menu of beef tips and chicken alfredo to barbecue chicken and pork. They had a great band and everyone really enjoyed the music, but it made for a longer than usual evening because the dancing went on so late. Ally texted Neal and let him know she might not make it to his place until after midnight. He texted back sad-faced emojis.

It was one-thirty before Ally drove up to Neal's. Everything was quiet. You could even hear the tide washing up on the shore. She tiptoed up the stairs to the kitchen door rather than using the elevator because she didn't want to wake Neal. She was sure he was dead asleep by now. He'd left a note on the counter telling her to just come to bed and she was happy to oblige.

Chapter - 31

Ally arrived at Marie and Larry's home at one o'clock. Real Mysteries had already had a few meetings with the Morgans, and had even sat down with Katie's brothers a few days ago, so this was merely a meeting to discuss the upcoming meeting with the Stricklands at their home in Syracuse and to find out more about Ally's role in the case.

Ally and Marie had decided beforehand that this was the time to share the letter Marie had found and where it had led Ally. "Marie probably already told you I was a year ahead of Katie at Syracuse and that I was also a nursing student. I remember when she went missing – it was pretty traumatic for all of us, especially since there were no leads and the police never found her, so when her remains washed up, I decided I wanted to help figure out what happened. I went to Syracuse to track down any information I could about a woman who wrote a letter to Katie that Marie only found a short time ago," she explained. "We now know, of course, that it was Anna Strickland who wrote the letter, but we didn't know that at the time. I found out that Katie had been volunteering at a shelter in downtown Syracuse and that's where she met Anna and her children. I even spoke to the woman who was the director at the time, and she remembered Katie very well, and how good she'd been to the Stricklands. I don't think you should mention the shelter's name or location, though, because abused women and children are still relying on the anonymity and security they find there. I also let Detective Hernandez at the Brunswick County Sheriff's Department know the name of the person. It was such old information, I'm not sure if they were able to do anything with it. I looked online myself but could not find any information. With only a name and no address you cannot do a lot. It is too common of a name."

Amy Gold nodded as she took notes.

"That's about the extent of my involvement, I'm afraid," said Ally. "Maybe Monica and Anna will be a bit more help," suggested Ally, and reached over to squeeze Marie's hand.

Chapter - 32

Real Mysteries arranged for the meeting with the Stricklands for the following Saturday afternoon. They would shoot several different segments there, but would try to keep the whole thing to under three or four hours. They suggested a camera-friendly wardrobe for the Morgans and Ally and said they'd have a make-up artist there as well. Unfortunately, Max Strickland, Anna's ex will not be present. He had a prior engagement.

Ally decided to wear one of the dresses she had left over from her New York dating scene days. She asked Mary if she would look in on Lucky, which Mary was happy to do, and Mary wished her luck with the interview.

"Hey, you're gonna be on TV! This is your fifteen minutes of fame, Ally!" she teased her.

Ally grimaced, then said, "I just hope it goes well and Anna and her family are everything we expect. Given the dangerous situation they were in and the fact that Katie helped them, it just seems like it could be connected to her murder."

She called Neal and brought him up to speed on the Katie saga. "Any chance you can come down the following weekend instead, since I won't be around next weekend?" she asked hopefully. He agreed to try.

The trip to Syracuse was tense. Ally and the Morgans flew into

JKF Airport and took a commuter to Syracuse. Ally rented a car and they arrived at the hotel by five o'clock on Friday, so Ally took them on a tour of Syracuse and the University district, where they had dinner at a Five Guys. By dinner's end, they were all exhausted and ready for bed.

After breakfast at the Tim Horton's located near the hotel the next morning, they went back to the hotel and dressed in their pre-approved apparel for being on the television show. They had to send pictures to the producer for her to approve all of it. She did not want any surprises. "Clothing matters on shows like ours. You would be surprised at what people think will look good on TV; we have a wardrobe department which we have to get approval for everything," she had told Marie before they left home. Ally drove them to 677 Cline St by using the navigation in the automobile. They had no problem and were impressed with the inviting and quiet little street with the tall oaks that seemed to give a kind of security blanket to the neighborhood. Ally could understand why Anna wanted to raise her children here.

Most of the Real Mysteries crew was already inside, other than the host, who would arrive later, but they saw Amy standing on the porch of the right side unit with a woman they knew was Anna. She was petite with short black, slightly graying hair. She smiled and Amy introduced them before they all moved inside. Amy introduced the cameramen and other crew members, including the makeup artist. Then Anna's daughters and their husbands appeared from next door and the introductions were completed. It was all fairly awkward, but Amy was skilled at making people feel at ease.

Anna addressed Marie and Larry. "I cannot thank you enough for raising such a wonderful daughter as Katie. She literally saved our lives."

Marie started crying and Anna hugged her close.

Ally teared up and asked the daughters, "'Do you both remember Katie?"

Monica nodded and smiled. "She helped me with my spelling and loved to play Barbie dolls with me."

Caroline said, "I was older so I remember her well. She was very kind to all of us."

Anna had prepared a light lunch for everyone of sandwiches, a fruit bowl and chips. She also had some lemon bars on a tray. "Mmm, my favorite," said Ally with a grin, remembering the ones Mary had brought to their first get-together.

As they ate, Anna and Marie spoke quietly, while Ally chatted with Caroline and Monica and their husbands talked to Larry. After lunch, it was time to get down to business.

Ally asked if she could use the bathroom to freshen up and Monica took her over to her house for some privacy. Ally wanted to brush her teeth, a habit she'd picked up during her nursing career. She never wanted to take care of patients with food in her teeth, and now she was going to be on TV, so food in her teeth would be mortifying! Monica, who was a soft-spoken young woman, asked Ally how she'd become involved in Katie's case. "I've heard bits and pieces, but is there more to the story?"

Ally told her the story from the beginning, when she'd seen the news report of Katie's remains on the beach near her home. "I had only recently moved into the house. It was surreal and brought me back thirty years to when she disappeared. I felt a kind of obligation to find out whatever I could. If I'd been living anywhere else, I doubt I'd be standing here right now, but that would be a shame," she said as she smiled at Monica.

As they returned to Anna's unit, Ally asked, "Would you tell me about Mrs. Lee? I'd love to hear about her."

"She was the sweetest, kindest person I have ever known. In fact, I named my daughter Eleanor after her. We call her Ellie. We were all very upset when she passed away, but she lived a wonderful, full life. She was a very spiritual person but not religious, in the sense she went to church regularly. She would take us on Easter and Christmas, though. We had her cremated according to her wishes. She's right up there on Mom's mantle," said Monica, pointing to a beautiful urn. *Good to know*, thought Ally wryly.

The host had arrived and they were ready to begin, so Amy had the makeup artist touch everyone up for the cameras, then asked Anna and her daughters to stand together as Marie and Larry approached them and they all hugged on camera. A few other shots were taken and then Amy directed them to the seats she had stationed for them around the cameras, though Caroline and Monica's husbands moved to the background.

The host was pleasant enough but didn't engage much with anyone and instead sat reviewing his notes. "He feels it makes the interviews seem more spontaneous," Amy explained. He sat down in a chair, with the families sitting on a sofa and other chairs facing him. It was set up very casually.

Chapter - 33

He first spoke with the Morgans about Katie and how her disappearance had changed their lives. He asked a little about who she'd been as a young woman and daughter. Both Marie and Larry teared up as they remembered their daughter. After a small break, it was Ally's turn to be interviewed and explain her role there. She went through the whole scenario of hearing about the washed up remains being identified as someone she had gone to school with and remembering when Katie had gone missing; she managed to contact Katie's parents and since they lived nearby, they got together.

The host paused and turned to Marie pointedly. He said, "And then I'm told you found… a letter. A very particular letter. Is that right?"

"Yes," Marie answered. "I found a letter Anna had written to Katie all those years ago."

The host turned to Anna. "You wrote to Katie after you'd moved into this home."

Anna said she'd contacted Rosie, the director of the shelter where she'd met Katie and asked her to pass on a letter of thanks. Katie had listed her parent's home address on her application, so that's where she sent the letter, but when Katie went missing, the letter was misplaced and forgotten about for thirty years.

Marie had brought the letter with her, and now she pulled it out of her purse and handed it to the host. The camera zoomed in on it and then he handed it to Anna. She took the letter out of the envelope and read it aloud. Tears were flowing by then and Amy called "cut."

They took a minute to gather themselves and the make-up artist touched up their makeup. When the camera started rolling again, the host asked the Morgans to explain how they found out Katie was missing.

Marie spoke about the anxious, terrifying days just before Thanksgiving, when they'd reported her missing, and no one had seen her in days. "The police in Syracuse interviewed everyone who knew her, but they had no leads," said Marie. "Students helped us hang flyers all around campus," added Larry. There was talk that there may be a serial killer in the area but it was way outside of Syracuse and they only had two women who were missing. The did not connect Katie's disappearance to the other case. "When Thanksgiving break was over and they were back at school, they held a vigil and hundreds of people attended. We were grateful, but no closer to finding her."

They both teared up again and the camera changed its focus to the host, who said, "I understand the police re-opened the cold case when Katie's remains were found, but their investigation has stalled without any new leads, is that right?"

The Morgans both nodded and Marie said, "It's been so long, they've told us not to get our hopes up. They now had a cold case unit that reviewed leads if they came in but there had not been anything until the remains washed up. They are hoping to get a lead after this show airs. They told us the serial killer that was a possibility so long ago was caught eventually and was found guilty and imprisoned, however he was killed in prison. So, if that would come up as a lead, we would probably never know for sure.

The host turned to Anna, who knew they wanted to hear about how she'd come to be at the shelter to meet Katie in the first place. At first she was reluctant to relive that awful time so long ago. She explained that she was married to a man that had become abusive towards her and he drank too much. "I was frightened of him and when he left and was gone for five days, leaving me with no way to contact him and very little money, I panicked and sought out the shelter. I felt terrible later and I did call him and reconciled with him up to a point. We did have a legal separation and then divorced. He has since remarried but he took care of his responsibilities with the children so everything turned out all right."

The host asked if anyone there had other suspicions about what happened to Katie that may or may not have been mentioned to the police?

Ally spoke up. "The shelter never contacted the police to tell them that Katie was a volunteer. They all seemed to believe there was no way Anna's husband could have known Katie had anything to do with his family, so they decided that sharing that information with police could have put the shelter's work at risk and endanger Anna and her children."

Anna interjected, "I didn't go to the police for the same reason. By the time we found out Katie was missing, I knew Max was probably back in town from his latest trip but I didn't see how he could have had any connection to Katie. And I was afraid of him, so I thought if I spoke to the police, he might find out where we were. It was a few weeks later that I contacted him and let him know where we were. I knew he would have been worried and hoped he would be conciliatory toward me by that time. He was and I was relieved. I never mentioned Katie to him but I believe the girls eventually told him about her, but I had kept her disappearance from them when they were so young. "

The room was silent. Ally felt like the camera stayed on Anna for a moment too long. Finally, Amy called "cut" and then announced, "I think we have everything we need. Thank you all very, very much. I know how hard all of this was on each of you."

The whole crew packed up in less than twenty minutes and the Morgans and Stricklands and Ally were left alone in Anna's home. They all hugged, thanked one another and bid farewell, promising to stay in touch if anything new happened.

Chapter - 34

Marie and Larry were exhausted and didn't want to go out to eat so they just drove back to the hotel. Before they left the house, Marie had hugged Anna several times and they exchanged phone numbers. Larry invited all of them to visit them in Myrtle Beach. "We can handle up to four people at a time," he said with a kind smile. They all thanked him for the generous offer and said they'd keep it in mind.

Back at the hotel, Ally ordered room service and they ate a light dinner and drank martinis as they discussed the day and how they all felt about it.

"I felt a little exposed," said Marie. "I didn't like being on television. Of course, our friends and family will all want to know every detail."

"Which you have probably already forgotten," Larry teased her.

Ally said, "I wonder if Anna told Max about the show and if he will watch it when it airs. He probably won't remember anything since he would not have known or have any idea about Katie, other than what the girls may have told him when they were young.

They were on a noon flight home the next day. Larry had kindly insisted on paying for the rental car even though Ally had told them she would cover it. As the plane took off, she looked down at the town where she had spent her college days. She could see how much it had grown in thirty years; nothing stays the same, she thought, especially relationships. She thought about the roommates she'd had during those years. She still kept in touch with one of them through email.

Deidra had been one of her best friends and was smart as a whip. She was sweet and kind and Ally knew immediately that she had the caregiver gift, as most good nurses do. She was African-American and had grown up in Harlem with a single mother and a little brother. She had helped raise her brother while her mother worked. Luckily, they saw their father on a regular basis and he was very attentive. Whenever he was able, he took her brother to Yankee's games, and took Deidra to museums, and both of them to the zoo and the occasional movie.

Deidra became very enamored with the arts. She could look at a painting and tell you exactly who'd painted it. She had a knack for it. Ally asked her one night why she had not chosen art as a career and she answered with a giggle, "Because I can't even draw a stickman!" They got a laugh out of that. "Besides, I always liked looking like a nurse, ya know? With the starchy uniform and that hat that made you look like *The Flying Nun.*" They laughed even harder at that.

Ally decided she was going to reach out to Deidra when she got home because Ally had never told her she'd moved, so they had a lot to catch up on. Deidra had moved to Atlanta after college and still worked at a hospital in the downtown area. Ally couldn't remember the name of it but she knew Deidra had met her husband there when he was a resident and they'd had three girls. Ally felt bad that they'd lost touch in the last couple of years and was definitely going to get in touch.

When they arrived in Wilmington, Larry got the car and on the ride home, Ally just laid back in the comfortable back seat and closed her eyes. Her nerves had been on edge for about two weeks and she was just now feeling like she was coming down from all that emotion. A nice relaxing bath was on the agenda when she got home. She called Mary to let her know she was on the way and Mary said she'd already taken Lucky home so he would be there to greet her. She thanked her and told her she was going to take it easy for a couple of days so she would skip tomorrow's trip to the gym.

She called work but got no answer, then remembered it was Sunday. Finally, she texted Neal and let him know she'd landed safely and they were driving home. She asked him to call her back tomorrow, and included a sleeping emoji.

As they dropped her off, Larry and Marie started talking about whether to stop for milk, and a few other groceries. Ally thought how impressive it was that they had just been through such a traumatic experience but could still talk about the menial day-to-day of their life. They were so comfortable with each other. She had read that there was a high divorce rate among couples who lose a child and asked them before getting out of the car, "How did you two hold up when Katie disappeared? I mean you're so close and obviously still in love. How did you get through it together?" She immediately stopped herself and said, "I'm sorry, I shouldn't ask such personal things. I'm not family and haven't known you long enough."

Marie smiled sadly and said, "Don't be silly, Ally, you're as close to us as family." She looked over at Larry and said, "We just 'soldiered on', as they say in England. It never crossed our minds that we would ever be apart. We had our sons to raise. Were we grief-stricken? Of course! We cried every night for months. In fact, sometimes we still catch each other crying, don't we, darling?" Larry nodded.

That was the end of it. Marie had explained that Larry was the love of her life and nothing would tear them apart, even the death of their daughter.

Chapter - 35

Ally was excited to see Lucky. She picked him up and cuddled with him as he purred loudly. He hung around her the rest of the evening, clearly having missed her. She felt drained of energy but managed to rustle up some eggs and toast. She started unpacking her suitcase when her cell phone rang. It was Neal. She answered, "I told you not to call" in a scolding voice.

He laughed. "You didn't really think I would obey you, did you?"

"No, I thought you might call."

"How are you, darling?"

Ally told him everything. She said there were a lot of tears.

Neal said he was proud of her for going through with it. "And who knows, something may come of it once it airs." Ally thought, *that's what I'm afraid of,* but didn't say it. He said he'd switched his schedule around and would be down Friday afternoon.

"I'll call Sara tomorrow to find out my schedule and I'll let you know. I can't wait to see you, sweetheart." They had been using endearments since their first night sleeping together and Ally liked it very much. Maybe she has turned the corner on her thoughts of settling down. Could it be? *Maybe I should see a shrink,* she thought seriously. She knew she had relationship issues.

Monday morning, she went for a walk on the beach. It was another Chamber of Commerce type of day, with blue skies and large cumulus clouds. She actually found a sand dollar. Maybe an omen? Good luck? She knew it was rare because they're so easily broken. At least she could add it to her collection.

When she returned home, she fed Lucky and cleaned out his litter box. "I'm so sorry, I had to leave you for a few days, Lucky honey. You're going to think Mary is your mother and I'm just your aunt!" She knew she sounded ridiculous but she couldn't help it – he was so adorable and she knew they had a bond.

She made a grocery list while she was enjoying her coffee and then remembered she wanted to get in touch with Deidre so she also wrote that down on her notepad of things to do. She wondered if Deidre had made it through the pandemic unscathed. She would call her later today.
She showered and dressed to go grocery shopping. She wanted to try and get on a budget and remembered an Aldi's nearby. The stock market was so volatile right now, it scared her. She was the old Ally, being frugal. She stocked up on fresh fruit and vegetables. She would share some of what she got with Mary so it wouldn't go bad. She also grabbed some dark chocolate. One square a day is all you need, she thought with a smile. She stopped at a carpet store on her way home, knowing she was going to have to replace the floors and carpet soon. She took a couple of samples and said she'd bring them back in a few days. She also made an appointment for them to come out to measure.

When she got home, she called Sara to see what they had on the books for her.

"We have a small birthday party on Wednesday night, if you're available; on Saturday we have a wedding reception in Leland."

"Okay, put me down for both. I'll stop by tomorrow and get any more future bookings so I can get back to work. I'm sorry I left you with so much."

Sara said, "Don't worry, we have your back, Ally." That was the nicest thing Sara had ever said to her, thought Ally with a grin.

She had a few hours before she planned to call Deidra, so she decided to start cleaning out the spare bedroom. She would separate anything personal that she thinks her mother or siblings might want and the rest would go to charity or a landfill. The bedroom had twin beds for the grandchildren when they visited. When they were really young, her grandparents would pull out a cot and all three kids would stay in the same room. There was a second guest room where Ally's parents stayed when they visited. Ally had taken over the master bedroom that had been her grandparent's room, since it was the largest and had a bathroom attached to it.

She cleaned out the single bureau, where she found some small soaps her grandmother had picked up over the years when she'd traveled. Since soap doesn't expire, Ally kept all of it. She didn't find any clothes. She threw out the liner paper and she dusted and polished the whole bureau. She would donate it to Habitat for Humanity. She did the same with the night stand. She found a letter in the top drawer that her sister Janet's husband, Adam, had written to Janet. It was out of the envelope so she had no idea when it had been written. She glanced at it but decided not to read it because it was personal. She put a post-it note on it with Janet's name.

She took a break to have a bite to eat. She'd been so caught up in cleaning that she'd forgotten to eat lunch! It was three-fifteen so she just had a piece of Jarlsberg cheese and a gala apple, her favorite.

Neal called and said he was beat; it had been a long day and wasn't over yet. He said he was on call that night so he had to go.

Chapter - 36

When Ally called Deidra late in the afternoon, Deidra answered right away. "Well, hello stranger," she greeted.

Ally apologized for letting so much time pass without getting in touch and asked her how she was.

"Well, to be honest, it's been a tough two years with the pandemic. I'd cut my hours a bit so I could finally have some time to myself now that only two of the girls are at home. But of course that changed when the pandemic hit and I was asked to work more hours. It was just expected, as I'm sure you know. But it's finally getting better now and I'm back to working just two days a week."

"That's good to hear. And how is Edward? He's an anesthesiologist, right? Are you both still at the same hospital?"

"Yes, both of us are still at Grady, the hospital where we met."

Ally said, "I know, how time flies, huh? As a matter of fact, I'm dating an anesthesiologist!"

"Really, you?" asked Deidre. "I remember you never wanted to date anyone you worked with, so how did that happen?"

"That's the thing," Ally explained, "I'm no longer a practicing nurse. I refused to take the vaccine so the hospital let me go and I moved to North Carolina. I don't know if you remember, but my grandparents had a beach house and it was passed on to my mother when my grandmother died. My family all agreed that I could move here since I was out of work and needed a place to live. It might even become my permanent home."

"Oh, I'm so sorry to hear that, Ally. You were the best nurse," said Deidre.

"Well, I had to make a decision so now I have to live with that decision. I actually got a job as a catering assistant and it's working out very well. Of course I'm not making near the money I was making as a nurse, but I don't need that much anyway. This place is paid for and I bought a car before I left New York, so financially I'm in good shape."

"I'm glad to hear that, you were always good with your money," recalled Deidre.

They continued to catch up. Ally wanted to know how old the children were now.

Deidre said, "You know we started late because Edward was still in school, so my oldest is 25, the middle one is 18 and the youngest is 13. She is the one I have to be home so much for; she does have a slight learning disability so having to do school online at home in her high school years was very tough on her. We hired tutors, though, and she came through it. Ally told her she understood now how busy she must be.

"I admire you for adjusting your career to help your children when they need it. Unfortunately, so many mothers don't have choices. The pandemic seems to have decimated the education of so many kids, it's tragic what they had to experience. It seems like so many will never get back the potential that was lost in the pandemic. I feel bad for that generation of kids. But it sounds like you managed to keep your daughter on course and succeeding, so good for you! You should be proud of yourselves too."

"Thanks, Ally, yeah, it was a challenge but I think we're through the worst of it finally. So what else is going on with you?"

"Well, there is something I wanted to tell you about, Deidre," said Ally.

"Ooo, this sounds rather ominous. What is it?"

"Do you remember the nursing student who went missing just before Thanksgiving in 1991?"

"How could I forget?" said Deidre. "It was all over the news, there were flyers everywhere and then there was that vigil, remember? What about her?"

"Well, you may or may not have heard that her remains washed up on a North Carolina beach recently. It was actually very near my house."

"Seriously?" gasped Deidre. "Do they know what happened to her?"

"No, not yet. But guess what? I've been involved in helping her parents. I found out they lived near me in North Myrtle Beach and felt compelled to get in touch with them to offer my condolences. Before I knew it, I found myself tied up in the mystery of what happened to Katie, their daughter. They're lovely people and I'm glad to help however I can. I've actually become a bit of a private detective, believe it or not!" she laughed.

"Wow, Ally, that's wild. But good for you for caring. I remember how sad it was that they never solved the case. It must've been awful for her family. Maybe now they'll at least have some resolution, right? And you've added a bit of excitement to your life, huh?" she said. "I mean, in addition to your new beau…" she laughed.

Ally promised to let her know how her new love life progresses. They even talked about getting together one day with their significant others. "Maybe we'll take a trip to Atlanta sometime. I'd love to see you and your family," she said, and Deidra agreed that would be wonderful.

Chapter - 37

The show was finally going to air that night. It had been four months since they had gone up to Syracuse. Actually, the producer told Marie that this is fairly fast compared t other shows they do. Ally spent the day expelling her nervous energy by cleaning her house. Janet called in the afternoon for a chat and said everything was fine with her and her family. Then she got to the point of her call. "Ally, I think Dad is getting Alzheimer's."

Ally was shocked. "Why do you say that? I was just there a little while ago and he seemed fine, just a little forgetful. Have you been around him recently?" asked Ally.

"No, but Mom called and she's concerned. And he's seeing a specialist. Nothing is confirmed but you know as a nurse how hard it is to diagnose."

"Yes, but the signs and symptoms are usually obvious and they can test them better now than they could a few years back. They're learning more and more about how to treat it. Still no cure, of course, but that's something."

Janet said, "Yes, I agree."

Ally decided to change the subject since there was not much more to talk about until they knew more. She asked about the kids, Justin and Rachel. "Well, as you know, Justin is graduating next year, thank goodness," she laughed. "And Rachel is great. She's not sure what she wants to do, though, so she's still at that community college. But maybe she'll follow in your footsteps and get a nursing degree," Janet said hopefully.

"She can't go wrong there," said Ally, although her enthusiasm for nursing had taken a hit lately. But she believed Rachel would make a wonderful nurse or any other kind of caregiver, for that matter. She was a gentle soul, Ally knew.

Ally asked about Adam, and Janet said he was working hard as usual. "He hopes to retire early, now that the kids are almost on their way."

It occurred to Ally that maybe they should have a family meeting about their father, or go see him or something, so she asked Janet what she thought.

"Mom said to wait until we normally go in July. By then, they'll know more. She also said they took out long-term healthcare insurance many years ago for something like this. She had one of her friends who's in insurance look at the policy and make sure it'll cover them if they have to put him in a long-term care facility in the future. Her friend said it would cover his needs."

Ally was suddenly overcome with melancholy. She felt awful for her mother. "I'll call Mom and hopefully speak with both of them. I don't keep in contact enough and that's on me. But will you keep me posted and let me know if there's anything I can do in the interim?"

Before they hung up, Ally told her sister about the Real Mysteries episode airing tonight and that she would be in it.

"Really, why?" Janet gasped.

"Do you remember when I was in college and a classmate went missing? Well, her remains washed up on a beach near the beach house. I reached out to her parents to offer my condolences because I knew the girl a little bit, and they asked me to help find more information on what happened to her. The police back then came up with nothing so it's been a cold case all these years, and now the police have no real leads."

"You were always the adventurous one, Ally. I don't mean that in a bad or mean way. I admire your tenacity, always have. I want you to know that."

"Thanks," was all Ally could say. "Would you call Mom for me to let her know about the show? I would hate for her to be watching and see me out of the blue. I haven't told her anything about any of this yet. You know what she would do." They both laughed, remembering how their mother wanted to know everything that was happening in their lives when they were younger.

"Sure, I'll call her, but don't forget to call them soon, okay? Or, well, she'll probably call you as soon as she watches the show!" she laughed. "Anyway, I'll be watching. Talk to you soon."

After they hung up, Ally just sat quietly and reflected about her parents and how much they meant to her, especially her dad. She knew more than her siblings would ever know about Alzheimer's. She'd had many patients over the years with it. She watched as their caregivers struggled to take care of them. The disease takes you from your life much sooner than death. Her father was going to be 81 on his next birthday. She had hoped her parents had crossed the line and escaped the disease, but she knew it was insidious and that her father may have had it for several years before it manifested itself. She knew he was bright and social enough to be able to hide any missteps he might have had. Eventually, though, you reach a point where you just can't hide it anymore.

She fed Lucky and cleaned out his litter box so Mary wouldn't have too much to do later tonight. She put on a light blue Talbot's blouse she'd found at one of the consignment shops and it still had the tags on it. She paired it with Chico's blue jeans and her least beat-up slides. Her hair had gotten long but after a good washing and blow drying it looked nice on her shoulders. She noticed crow's feet around her eyes and thought maybe she should look into Botox. There were several places in the area that advertised it. *Or was she being vain?* she wondered. Probably.

She heard the horn blow and gave Lucky a kiss and said she would see him in the morning. She picked up her overnight bag she had started keeping ready for occasions such as this and the basket with the salad and dressings she'd prepared and headed out the door.

Mary was happy to see her. "So, are you nervous?" she asked.

"A little," Ally admitted. Mary had her Sirius radio tuned to her favorite station 'Seriously Sinatra', so they drove to Neal's listening to Ol' Blue Eyes, who could belt out a song like no one else, except Michael Bublé, thought Ally with a smile.

Neal welcomed them and gave Mary a hug before hugging and kissing Ally. "I feel like I've known you forever," Neal said to Mary with a wink.

"I feel the same," she said sweetly.

A few minutes later Marie and Larry arrived with two large pizzas from a local Italian restaurant. They smelled incredible. Ally served up her salad and Neal had a bottle of chardonnay and a bottle of chianti opened for them. Neal and Larry talked sports. They both had their favorite teams and were judging their chances for the upcoming season. Mary, Marie and Ally tried to keep the conversation light because they knew what was coming. Ally asked Marie if she thought Anna and her family were going to watch.

"Yes, she called me this afternoon. She seems nervous now about doing the show. She just hopes there's nothing in it that will upset her ex, now that they were on amicable terms, she would not want anything to upset him. The children are grown now and things are much better.

As showtime approached, everyone took a seat in front of the large TV in the great room. Marie had Larry on one side and Ally on the other as they all waited with nervous anticipation.

Chapter - 38

The opening scene was of Monica and Anna walking arm-in-arm up the sidewalk and into the gate of the white fence Anna had installed after Eleanor Lee had passed. Eleanor never wanted a fence because she felt it was unwelcoming. Anna, on the other hand, did not want to welcome anyone so she made that decision. She did have the house number 677 added to the post of the gate, which was caught by the cameraman as he followed the women up to the house.

Everyone was spellbound watching part of the people in this room on the large TV screen. It was surreal, Ally would comment later. All in all it seemed to capture the solemness of the situation and the warmth of the families finally meeting one another.

When the show ended, Marie and Larry were holding each other close. Ally knew how difficult it must have been to relive their daughter's disappearance and then hear about the discovery of her remains all over again, then listen to people speculate about Katie's movements in her final days.

Marie and Larry were ready to head home. They needed some alone time and probably wanted to call their sons, who'd been watching from their own homes. Mary was right behind them. She told Ally she would look in on Lucky before going home and would stop in and feed him in the morning. She leaned in and told her quietly to "take your time getting home," and winked.

There wasn't much cleaning up to do but Ally tidied up because she needed to stay busy. Neal suggested they go for a walk on the beach. There was a full moon and the beach was crowded. Apparently, there was a group that held full moon parties. They walked in the opposite direction and held hands. Neal said, "I know that was hard to watch.

"Come here," he said as he led her to the other side of someone's walkway, where they were in complete darkness. He put down the beach mat he had grabbed before leaving and helped her down onto it. Before she knew it, she was helping him remove her shirt and her jeans were unzipped and half way down. He helped her with the other half.

After they made love, they just spooned each other for a while. He covered her nakedness with both of their shirts. There was no one on this end of the beach. Because of the sea turtle restrictions, no one turned on their back lights at night. The moon was their only source of illumination. Ally said, "I feel like a teenager."

"Wow, you were doing this in your teens?" he quipped. She jabbed him in the shoulder. *If he only knew,* she thought with a secret smile.

They dressed and walked back to his house. They were both still restless and not ready for bed so Neal opened another bottle of chardonnay and they sat on the back deck. The breeze from the sea was gentle and it was a bit humid.

"Do you really want to know about my first time?" Ally asked. "I'll tell you mine if you tell me yours," she teased.

"Okay, go," he said.

"Well, I was sixteen. I'd been seeing a boy in my class for about six months when we went to the school's proverbial Valentine's Day dance. We double-dated with a couple who'd brought a bottle of Jim Beam. I had never had alcohol before and was reluctant but they poured some in my Coca-Cola and the next thing I knew I woke up in the back seat of my boyfriend's car."

Neal sat up and said "What?"

"Yes, it's true. I had a date rape drug put in my drink. I didn't remember a thing and was so dazed when I woke up, I had no idea what had happened. My boyfriend admitted to me that we had sex but said he'd used a condom. He told me I was all over him and he was happy to do it, too. It was apparently his first time as well. I was so young. I didn't know people did those things to other people, drugging, I mean. I guess I was lucky they didn't take pictures like they do to girls today. At least social media wasn't around in the '80's."

"Did you tell your parents?" asked Neal.

"Oh, absolutely not!" exclaimed Ally. "My mother would not have believed me and it would've killed my father. I just figured if he really did use a condom then at least I wouldn't get pregnant. He apologized over and over again but I broke up with him and never spoke to him again. As far as I know, he never told anyone either. I was never sure if that creep we double-dated with knew what had happened. I dropped them both as friends and the guy eventually transferred to another school."

There was a brief silence as Neal absorbed Ally's story.

"Your turn," said Ally, wondering if he had anything so shocking to offer.

"Mine is boring in comparison. I went to Catholic schools all of my life and married my college sweetheart."

Ally laughed. "Yes, compared to me, I guess that is boring. But I would take boring anytime over what I went through." When Neal didn't say anything, she followed up with, "I take it your college sweetheart was your first?"

Neal said, "Yes. And I was monogamous right up to the divorce and for six months afterwards. I found her with someone else. Not with just anyone but with our neighbor from across the street."

Ally could see the pain and sadness on Neal's face. "Oh my, that must've been awful. I'm sure it was a hard time to go through. I'm so sorry."

He thought about it and said, "As I look back on it, I can see that our marriage came apart when our son graduated high school and went to college. We realized we had nothing in common. Of course, I didn't expect to have it end the way it did. It unnerved me and I wasn't able to talk about it for a very long time. I hid it from our son for his sake. I don't think he ever needs to know what the trigger was for our separation, just that we drifted apart."

"That's probably a good idea," said Ally. "I never really wanted children. I could never figure out why but after telling you my story tonight, I think I just couldn't bear anything happening to my child like what happened to me."

Eventually they went to bed and just cuddled all night. Ally felt security like she'd never felt before.

Part - 3

Chapter - 39

Max and Anna
1981

Max Strickland did not have a difficult upbringing. He was the fourth son of eight children. He grew up in Oneida, New York in a big Irish Catholic family. His father worked at the Oneida Silver plant. They were lower middle class but never wanted for anything. His mother did not work outside the home. They always had enough to eat. Christmas was the best time. They had to share some toys but there was at least one thing he got that he wanted. He remembered getting his own BB gun when he was about eleven.

When Max reached eighth grade, he started getting into trouble. He fell in with the wrong crowd. At first he would be late coming home after school, but it eventually progressed to his grades declining. His parents gave him the usual speech about school, the importance of getting good grades and of "making something" of himself. His problem was that he had a bit of a lazy streak. He was slow at his chores and sometimes 'conveniently' forgot to do them.

He struggled along in school and managed to graduate high school. He didn't have the grades or the desire to go to college, or even a trade school, though, so he worked menial jobs. For a while he worked at the local pizza joint because he didn't have to get up early and he enjoyed the delivery part of it. He found he really liked to drive and learned the streets pretty easily. At some point, he began thinking that truck driving might be a better fit for him. He found out you didn't need a college education to work for a trucking company and that they would send you to a school for training.

He opted to work for a local moving company instead because he wasn't sure about the school thing. His lazy streak was not improving. After working there for a year, he applied for a job as a bus driver with Syracuse Transit. He had to get a special license but that was not a problem. He liked the job and was making enough money to move into an apartment of his own.

He had been living with his older brother, Steve, who he could tell was ready to be rid of him. Besides, he thought, maybe his love life would improve once he had his own place. He started going out more and hanging out at the bars. He always watched what he drank because a DUI would be an automatic termination. He worked from six a.m. to three p.m. and had an hour for lunch, but he didn't need it. He would get to the bar by four but never stayed past eight. Strict rule. He met a lot of women there and a few he even brought back to his place, but he was never serious about any of them. None of them were the type to take home to Mother.

One day a petite woman got on his bus at around noon. She had a short 'bob' haircut and beautiful blue eyes. She sat on the first seat behind the door, opposite from him. He could see her pretty legs out of the periphery of his right eye. Every time he made a stop to let someone on or off, he would turn ever so slightly so he could see her better. Unfortunately, it was close to his lunchtime and another driver would be taking over at the next stop. He only hoped she would be a regular and he could start up a conversation the next time.

He was thrilled when the next day she got on at the same stop. He knew he had to make conversation with her before his lunchtime came up. Once she sat down, it would be too late, he thought. But then, out of the blue, she initiated conversation by asking if there was a sandwich shop at the corner of Abernathy and Coolidge, where she gets off. He turned a little toward her and said there was and that in fact he usually ate there on his lunch hour. He said he would be happy to show her. She smiled in agreement. He figured she thought he was respectable because he had a uniform on. So, they got off at the stop and his replacement boarded. This was his lucky day, he realized, as their schedules changed daily depending on call offs, so he was pleased that he was replaced at the same stop where Anna got off.

He introduced himself to her and she did the same. "I'm Anna Turner," she said. They walked another half block to Cheeky's Deli. Max told her they had the best pastrami sandwiches around.

She said, "I think I'll do something a little lighter. I have a job interview today and don't want to have pastrami hanging in my teeth."

Max howled at that. "Then I would just get a bowl of their delicious broccoli and cheese soup. You can't go wrong with that." They placed their order at the counter, then chose a table and waited for their number to be called.

"I really appreciate you going out of your way," Anna said with a shy smile. "I hope I'm not keeping you from anything."

Max assured her it was nice to have someone to eat with for a change. He asked her where she was from.

"I grew up in Danville but moved here a year ago to take a course in data entry and Executive Assistance, which used to be secretarial training."

"That sounds interesting," Max said. "You must have been a good student. I was never very good in school and was especially not good at math. Driving a city bus is about my skill level," he said self-deprecatingly. "Maybe it's a confidence thing, I dunno. My mother always encouraged me but my dad was not a great influence. I don't mean to speak badly of him, though. He did his best. We were never without a home or food, so I can't complain."

Anna nodded, "I'd really like an office job. I worked in a textile mill back home but they closed and moved operations to China. It's either learn a skill and get a job or starve," she laughed. Then she added, "You should be proud of your job. After all, how would people get around without bus drivers? Plus all the ones I've seen have been really friendly and kind to passengers." She chuckled nervously.

Max decided he was really enjoying talking with her. Their food came and they ate heartily. Anna told him how good the soup was and thanked him for recommending it. "And it's all I really need, because my stomach has butterflies," she confessed.

Max told her she would knock them dead and he was sure she would get the job. He then asked her if he could see her again.

She said, "That would be nice," and she gave him the phone number of the home where she was renting a room from a woman. She was only allowed to receive one or two calls a week but she could make as many outgoing local calls as she wanted. The woman was pleasant enough, she just didn't want to become Anna's social secretary, she'd told her. "But don't call after nine o'clock at night. She goes to bed around then and would be irritated if she got a call." Then she said in a hushed tone, "I'm looking forward to moving out and finally getting a place of my own."

Max had insisted on picking up the check. He said he would call her in the next few days and he meant it. She thanked him again and went on to her job interview. What Max didn't know at the time was that she was thinking, *I believe I just had lunch with my future husband.*

Chapter - 40

Max felt great after lunch with Anna. He realized he had his own butterflies. Could it be love? He got off at three and went to his favorite bar. He knew he was getting a little too used to the drink and did not think Anna would approve of that part of him. He decided this was going to be his last night of having too much fun. After all, it was Friday so he could sleep in tomorrow morning. He saw one of his favorite redheads and walked over to where she was sitting at the bar. "Wanna have a little fun tonight?" he asked.

"Sure, if you're buyin'," replied Vicki.

"We can do more than that if you're game," said Max flirtatiously.

By midnight, they'd both had quite a bit of liquor and very little food, and caught a cab to his place. Max was looking forward to releasing some sexual tension and apparently Vicki was also in the mood. Before his apartment door shut, she had her blouse and bra off and was working on her skirt. Shoes went flying. He was frantically removing his shirt and she was helping him with his pants. Before he knew it, she was giving him the prerequisite blow job. Then it was his turn and they headed to the bedroom.

The next morning, he woke with a killer headache. There was a note on the pillow next to him that said, "I had to get home in time for my son to be dropped off from his sleepover. Thanks for the great night. Hope we can repeat it sometime."

Max knew it was his 'coup de gras'. He was through with drinking and loose women. He had his sights on Anna Turner. He was going to turn his life around starting today. After coffee and two extra strength Excedrin, he showered and dressed. He headed to the local barbershop and got a nice haircut. He went to Sears and bought a couple pairs of dress pants, two dress shirts and three new ties. He also went to the shoe department and bought a new pair of dress shoes. He wanted to look nice for Anna. He'd grown up Catholic, and even though they hadn't discussed it, he suspected she might have also. He was even going to go to confession later that day. He would call her on Monday to see how her interview had gone and ask her out again.

Monday morning came and he was on his first break. He used the pay phone and called Anna. "So how did the interview go on Friday?" he asked when she came to the phone.

"I got the job!" she said excitedly.

"Congratulations, that's wonderful, Anna! I'm really happy for you. When do you start?"

"This Thursday he wants me to come in for two days of orientation and I officially start on Monday. I'm so excited, Max. I can't wait."

"Well, how about we celebrate tonight?" Max suggested, holding his breath as he waited for her answer.

"I need to do some apartment hunting today. I guess I could meet you someplace later. Would that be okay?"

"Absolutely," said Max, unable to keep the grin off his face. They made arrangements to meet at a Steak and Ale downtown. Anna would take the bus but Max would offer to take her home. She sounded like she was feeling very good about seeing him tonight.

Anna lined up some appointments to look at rental apartments close to where she was currently living. Once she got a car, she could move closer to her new job but for now she would need to stay near a bus line. She had looked at three places by eleven-thirty. None had been right for her. She wanted a one bedroom, one bath with some kind of porch or patio. She also wanted to be able to have a cat for company but all the places she'd seen had a no pets sign posted. This was harder than she thought it would be. Her next appointment was at one o'clock so she walked home and got a snack from her room.

The landlady allowed a small heating element in the room to heat up soup or boil a pot for tea. Anna had some tuna, so she mixed it up with some mayonnaise and relish packets she'd collected and made herself a sandwich. She looked through her closet for a dress to wear for her date that night. She had only been buying work clothes for a while, so she didn't really have evening wear but she did have one dress she used on special occasions, like for church or funerals. It was deep purple with a V-neck and three-quarter-length sleeves. It really showed off her petite figure. She had a string of pearls and matching earrings that she knew would look nice. But then she changed her mind and decided that would look too 'church-like' and decided on another necklace that hit just above her cleavage. It was a heart with rhinestones but they looked real. She would wear her diamond stud earrings her mother gave her when she graduated high school. She had a black pair of shoes that looked dressy, not business-like. She thought that would be appropriate for a nice steak restaurant with a man she wanted to impress. She remembered the phrase 'dress to impress', but couldn't remember where she'd heard it.

Anna freshened up and went back out, on her way to the next apartment, which was just three blocks west of her current place. The landlady was very nice and showed Anna a one-bedroom unit that had just become available. It still needed painting and carpet cleaning, but the kitchen was large enough for a small table and two chairs. Off the living room were sliding doors that led to a small patio with a railing. She loved it but asked about whether she could have a cat. The landlady said cats and small dogs were allowed and that there was a pet deposit. No more than one animal, though.

"When could I move in?" she asked eagerly.

"It'll be ready by next Monday," she assured Anna.

"Perfect," said Anna. "I'll take it." She completed the application and paid the landlady the deposit and the first month's rent. She explained she'd be moving her things from her mother's home in Danville with a U-Haul so wouldn't be moving in until late in the week after it was ready. "Could I move in next Saturday if I can get help moving my things then?"

"Of course, that's not a problem," said the landlady. "Just stop by for the keys and I'll show you where you can park out back to unload."

Anna arrived at seven o'clock at the Steak and Ale restaurant to find Max waiting for her at the front entrance. He'd already informed the maître 'd that he was meeting a lady. They were quickly seated at a romantic table for two.

Max smiled broadly and said, "Wow, you look great, Anna."

She thanked him and complimented him on his attire. "You look different out of your uniform," she joked.

"That's good, right?" he responded as they both laughed. "Tell me how your apartment hunting went?"

"Very well!" she replied excitedly. "As a matter of fact, I put down a deposit and first month's rent on a really cute one bedroom on King St. I hope to move in next Saturday. I have to go to my mother's and pack up some things and then rent a U-Haul and see if my brother-in-law is available to help me move, but I'm really looking forward to having my own place."

"I can help you move," Max said quickly. "I'd be happy to."

"Really? Oh, Max, that is so nice of you. Are you sure you want to spend your weekend helping someone move?" asked Anna with a grimace.

"Why not? I don't have anything else more pressing and you're kind of important to me, if you don't mind me saying so. I like to help my friends."

Anna blushed and accepted his generous offer. She really liked this new man in her life.

So, on the following Saturday she and Max drove to her mother's house in Danville and rented a U-Haul that Max could hitch to his car, since he already had a hitch applied from his move to Syracuse. The whole ordeal took less than eight hours and they had all her things moved into her new apartment. They were both exhausted. Since the phone had not yet been installed, they couldn't call for food to be delivered, so they decided to go out for pizza and beer. They really enjoyed each other's company. Max was a perfect gentleman. He had really impressed her mother, who was a hard person to impress. Her father had died years ago and Anna's mother had been making the decisions for the family ever since.

Anna woke up on Sunday glowing. She was in her element. She was excited about starting her job the next day. She had gone through two days of orientation last Thursday and Friday so she felt ready and anxious to start tomorrow. She was so glad Max had been able to help her move. Everything was coming together nicely.

She didn't have that much furniture, so she'd work on filling out the furniture by going to Goodwill stores whenever she could. Today she was going to an animal shelter to adopt a cat. She'd already checked their hours and they were open on Sundays from one to four. They told her they included a temporary cardboard carrier with all adoptions if an adopter needed one to take a cat home. Their cats were all spayed and neutered before they adopted them out, but this fee was included in the adoption fee.

There were many beautiful cats to choose from and she would have taken them all if she could. She found a black and white kitten that had been there for two weeks. The mother had been killed and her kittens had been found nearby and brought to the shelter. All of its littermates had already been adopted but this little guy had a deformed foot. The shelter told Anna that the vet thought it was a birth defect, but the little kitten could walk just fine regardless.

She took a cab home because she didn't think buses would allow an animal, plus she didn't want to jostle the sweet little kitten more than necessary. She had already purchased cat food and arranged to take him to a vet for a thorough check-up. The shelter said she'd be responsible for getting him up to date on shots. She had also bought some water and food bowls, a bunch of toys and a litter box and litter from her local pet store during the week. Now all she had to do was name him. She'd seriously considered Max a while ago but now that she was coincidentally dating a Max, she thought that was a bad idea. She decided on Moe, one of the Three Stooges, her father's favorite show, and little Moe became her constant companion.

Chapter - 41

Anna started her new job the next morning. She was in a pool of people doing data entry. It was mundane but it was a start, and with some experience she figured she would move up and maybe even apply for a better job. She really wanted to be an Executive Assistant (a glorified secretary, her mother called it), but knew it would take time. She wanted to see Max again. Since he couldn't call her because she didn't yet have a phone installed, he told her to call him tonight so they could catch up.

She got off at five o'clock and was home forty-five minutes later. She went to the pay phone at the corner and called Max right away but there was no answer. She briefly wondered where he was but then told herself it was none of her business. She'd try again later. The phone company couldn't install her phone until the following week because she needed them to come in the evening when she was home.

Anna and Moe were quickly bonding. He seemed to be enjoying his new abode. She'd forgotten to get him a bed so she put down an old pillow for him to sleep on during the day, but he found all sorts of places to sleep, including her own bed, which was fine with her. She was relieved to see he had a good appetite and seemed to be healthy but she'd made a vet appointment for Saturday in two weeks to get him his shots and have him looked over.

She began unpacking; before she knew it, it was dark outside, so she decided against calling Max again tonight. She was exhausted and just wanted to get some sleep and be well-rested for tomorrow. She and Moe were cuddled up in bed and asleep by nine. She dreamed of a noisy office and running her fingers across a keyboard all day.

The next day Anna arrived at work fifteen minutes early and stopped in the break room for a cup of coffee. She had only instant coffee at home because she hadn't bought a coffee pot yet. There was a woman named Barbara there and they started chatting. Barbara said she'd started two weeks ago, was from Buffalo and recently divorced. "Thank goodness we didn't have children," she shared with Anna. "He cheated on me." Anna was pleased to have met someone she liked so quickly and the two women talked about trying to schedule their lunch together. They were only given forty-five minutes, as well as two fifteen minute breaks during the day.

Since Anna hadn't been grocery shopping yet, she didn't have enough food at home to bring her lunch, so she had to run out to the corner deli, but it took so long to get through the line that by the time she got back to the break room, she only had about ten minutes to eat. She decided she'd get off the bus on the way home to pick up some groceries. Her first paycheck wasn't until next Friday, so she was very glad she'd lived at home until recently so she could save money. Luckily, the job paid very well. She believed she would be able to move up in the company because she finally had some skills. The company also encouraged employees to enroll in the local community college, and had programs to help with tuition. She made a mental note to look into it.

She stopped by the market but knew she wouldn't be able to carry everything she needed because she had to walk three blocks to her apartment. She hoped to start looking for a car soon so she wouldn't have these problems.

As she walked up to her building, loaded down with as much as she could manage, she saw Max standing outside waiting for her. She smiled with surprise, but instead of returning her smile and saying hello, he said, "Where have you been?" He seemed to quickly realize he was being rude and presumptuous, and added, "I've missed you," and took some of the shopping bags from her.

Anna said she'd tried calling him last night but there was no answer. "You should get an answering machine," she suggested. She told him how her first day at work had gone and that she'd started unpacking last night and went to bed early. "Moe and I were just exhausted," she laughed.

Max helped her put away her groceries and offered to take her to Walmart the coming weekend so she could stock up on whatever she needed, including a coffee pot. "I'll buy it for you as a housewarming present," he smiled sweetly.

Anna offered to make him a sandwich but he admitted he'd stopped at the bar for a beer and a sandwich before coming over. She made herself a grilled cheese and they both sat on the sofa, as Max held and petted Moe. She told him all about her job, about meeting Barbara and about her aspirations to take additional courses that would help her move up in the company.

"Do you just want to work the rest of your life?" he asked. "I mean, don't you want to get married and have kids eventually?"

She said, "Sure, when I find the right man," and smiled shyly.

They sat silently for a few moments and then Max asked, "Would I be in the running?"

She took a second too long to answer and he seemed to be wondering why, so she decided to be straight with him. "Listen Max, I do like you a lot, really. You've been very good to me. But I just got out of a rocky relationship with someone I worked with back home and need some time to process everything. You understand?"

Max looked relieved and said, "Of course I do, Anna. I'm glad you told me and that's why you looked so unsure instead of giving me the brush-off I was bracing for," he joked.

Anna decided he was a great guy.

They made plans to go out to breakfast on Saturday morning then go shopping. "I'm gonna get a newspaper and start looking for a car. Can you help me?"

"I'd be happy to. Don't worry, we'll get you fixed up. It's none of my business, I know, but do you wanna tell me how much you wanna spend?"

"I have $5,000 but am hoping to spend less, if possible."

"Gotcha," Max nodded. He said goodbye to Moe and kissed Anna on the lips for the first time as he left. "I'll see you on Saturday at nine a.m."

After Max left, Anna pulled out her Bible and read from Psalms, something she tried to do every night. She had set herself a goal to get through Psalms and Proverbs by the end of the year, so she had five months to go. She wasn't a regular churchgoer, of course. Growing up, her family had only gone to church at Easter and sometimes Christmas. Her Biblical knowledge was lacking and she wanted to know more. She'd realized this during her last relationship. She'd met Jeff at the plant where she worked in Danville. She was nineteen when she started working there and was naive when it came to men. Her mom had been very strict with her and hadn't allowed Anna to start dating until she was sixteen, and she always had an eleven o'clock curfew. She also couldn't go out on weeknights because her mother worked and needed to get to bed early.

Anna's older brother, Hugh, had been a lot to handle for her mother. He was very handsome, like her late father, and had girls coming by and calling all the time. It was hard to keep him out of trouble. He was a good brother, though. She went to him for advice on boys and he was always looking out for her best interests. Her older sister, on the other hand, had become pregnant in high school and got married the weekend after she graduated. Luckily, she married a great guy, but that was part of the reason Anna's mother was so watchful over her. Her sister, Audrey, lived near their mother and had two more children after having Troy right after high school. Audrey's husband, Dale, was a plumber and works for his father while Audrey stays home and raises the children, just like she always wanted. Anna was pleased that they were doing very well and that Dale was a good man. He would take over his father's business when he retired, so they had a long-term plan, which Anna knew was important for such a large family.

Chapter - 42

Saturday arrived quicker than Anna could have imagined. Between work and unpacking, she'd been very busy all week and was having trouble catching up on her sleep. She couldn't wait to have her phone installed next Saturday so she could call her family and let them know how she was doing.

Max arrived right at nine o'clock as promised. She felt a little bad about leaving Moe after working all week, but would spend tomorrow at home and give him some extra attention. They stopped at an IHOP for breakfast and as they ate, Anna showed him a few car ads she'd found in the newspaper. He thought a couple of them sounded promising, so they'd call about them after shopping. There was a Ford Fairmont with low mileage at $4200. "It probably belonged to a little old lady who died," he chuckled.

Anna just stared at him. "That isn't funny."

He looked up from his pancakes and saw she was serious. "Oh geez, I'm sorry, Anna. I was just jokin' around."

Anna sighed. "Oh, I'm sorry, Max, I guess I need to lighten up a bit. It's just been a hectic week and I feel like I can't turn off from work. Data entry can really get on your nerves, to be honest."

Max seemed relieved that she'd forgiven him so quickly. He paid the tab again. He was very gentlemanly with her, always opening doors and making sure she was comfortable with the air conditioning in the car. They arrived at the Walmart and it felt like they were a married couple, as Anna consulted her list and checked prices. She was very careful with her money. After she'd finished with groceries, she went to the pet aisle and found a nice bed for Moe, along with another toy.

Max helped her pick out a coffee pot. She chose a Mr. Coffee because that's the one her mother had. On the drive back to her apartment, she asked Max if she could make him dinner that night and he said that would be great. He was going to call the car ads for her when he got back to his apartment and wanted to know when she'd be able to go look at them. She said she could go tomorrow if it worked out for the sellers. She didn't like the idea of leaving Moe again but having a car was important now.

Max returned at six-thirty with a bouquet of flowers. She beamed and told him how sweet it was, but said she didn't even have a proper vase yet, and realized she should have brought one from her mom's, who had several stored under the kitchen sink. For now, Anna pulled out her tallest drinking glass and arranged them in there, then set them on her coffee table. They would also be using the coffee table to eat because she hadn't purchased a kitchen table yet.

She made spaghetti since that was her best dish. Her mother had taught her how to make it when she was twelve and it had always been her favorite. She had even purchased a bottle of red wine to go with the meal and they enjoyed the wine so much they finished the bottle. She had not made a dessert. She'd completely forgotten. "I'm so sorry, Max, I rarely eat dessert, so it didn't cross my mind."

Max didn't seem to mind in the slightest. "Anna, the meal was delicious and I'm not big on dessert either. This country eats way too much sugar and everyone's getting fat," he frowned. Anna put his comment in her mind's rolodex. *Hmm…don't get fat,* she thought to herself.

She didn't have a TV yet, either. She could have brought the one from the guest bedroom at home but she knew her mother let the grandchildren use it for their videos so she hated to take it from them. She told Max a TV would come after the car. He said he didn't mind. He helped her do the dishes and then they just sat on the couch, a little closer than usual. She was becoming very comfortable with him being there, but she wasn't ready to take it any further and she sensed he knew that. At ten-thirty, he said he should probably get going but would be back tomorrow at one and would hopefully have a couple of appointments lined up to see cars.

After he left, Max made a beeline to his local bar. Anna was on his mind but he was in need of something else right now. He could tell by her body language she was not ready to hop in the sack, but he was. Luckily, one of his casual hookups was sitting at the bar. "Hey, Tammy."

Tammy turned and raised her eyebrows as she greeted, "Hey stranger. Where've you been? Haven't seen you in a while."

Max ordered a beer and responded, "Well, you see me now, so whaddaya say?"

"Let's go," shrugged Tammy happily, as Max downed his beer. She grabbed his hand and they headed for the exit.

Chapter - 43

Max awoke around nine. He looked over at Tammy sleeping beside him. He went to the bathroom and when he came out, she was lying on her side facing him. "Up for round three?" she asked playfully.

As much as he loved her body, he knew he had turned a corner. Anna was constantly on his mind. He was torn between wanting sex with this woman in his bed and holding back because he thought he might be falling in love with another woman.

"Sorry Tammy but I've got a lot to do today. We should probably call it off for now."

She looked disappointed but she could see he was being sincere, so she gathered her clothes and went to the bathroom to dress. She gave him a kiss on the cheek as she left the apartment. "See ya 'round, Max," she winked. The tequila shots he'd had with Tammy last night had caused a bit of a hangover, so Max downed a couple of aspirin with his coffee and toast. At eleven-thirty he called about the Ford Fairmont. An elderly-sounding woman with a sweet voice answered. This'll be easy, thought Max. He asked if the car was still available and she said absolutely, then they discussed the mileage and model. She said it was a 1978 but wasn't sure about the mileage.

"It belonged to my late husband and I already have a car," she explained.

Max said he understood and asked if he and his girlfriend could come see it later that day. She told him any time would be fine. He asked if today would be too much of an imposition since both he and his girlfriend worked. He repeated that they were both very interested and would pay cash. She said today would be fine and they settled on four o'clock.

Max arrived at Anna's at one and told her they had an appointment to see the Ford Fairmont at four o'clock. She was pleased but admitted she couldn't pay the full price today and hoped the seller might accept a deposit or hold her check until she could transfer money into her checking account. Max didn't think it would be an issue.

Since they had time to kill, they went to Target and Anna picked up a few things for the kitchen. She also looked at televisions and decided to get a small Emerson. She needed something to watch at night and especially when Max was over because he enjoyed watching sports.

They arrived at four and the woman selling the car introduced herself and took them to the garage to see it. It was in excellent condition. "My husband was retired and really never drove it much," she explained.

Max checked the mileage: only 28,000. He checked the tires and looked under the hood. He asked the last time it was driven and she said her neighbor had taken it out once a week just so the battery would not go bad. Max asked for the keys. He wanted to back it out of the garage to check for steering problems and to check the floor for oil leaks. He found no issues at all. He and Anna spoke quietly off to the side.

"How do you like it, babe?" he asked her.

" I like the color." It was midnight blue with soft blue seats. She looked through the entire inside and could not find a tear or stain anywhere. She checked for smoke and any other smells but found nothing off-putting.

She told Max, "I like it a lot and would be willing to pay the whole $4200 if she'll take a deposit or hold a check for three or four days until I can transfer the rest from my savings account."

Max would have offered the woman $3800 but Anna had softened him. She was a sweet little lady and could probably use the extra cash. Besides, she wasn't asking too much in the first place.

Anna made her offer and the woman said she would be happy to take a deposit or post-dated check as long as Anna provided her with her employment details and contact information. "You'll have to get insurance on it immediately, of course. And as soon as the check clears, I'll mail you the deed or you can stop by and pick it up, but you can take the car now," she said.

Anna beamed at her with gratitude.

"It has a full tank of gas!" added the elderly woman.

"Sweet," said Max, nodding.

Anna drove the car home as Max followed. She felt very independent. She was so very appreciative of everything Max had done for her.

When she got home, she parked in a lot across from her apartment building. She knew she would have to get a pass and pay a monthly parking fee but didn't want to leave her car on the street. She parked in the visitor spot for now and would talk to the super when she got inside. Max had parked on the street nearby and helped her carry everything inside. After they'd unloaded everything, Anna ran down to the super's apartment to tell him about the car and he told her to call the office tomorrow and they would arrange for her to get a sticker. She thanked him and ran back up to her apartment, where Max was waiting.

Chapter - 44

Anna put away her new things as Max took the TV out of the box and managed to get a local station with the antennae. A football game was on. She was not really into sports but Max watched it for a while. She used the tuna and noodles she had to make a casserole, which turned out better than she'd expected. She added rolls and some canned peaches to the meal, which they ate on the coffee table as Max continued watching the game. Afterwards, he helped her with the clean-up, and then they sat on her sofa and began kissing. Max decided to get a little more aggressive with his groping, so he started kissing her neck and reached into her blouse. Anna did not resist. She had feelings for Max. She wondered if he thought she was a virgin, even though she'd told him about a past relationship.

She'd dated a guy named Ben, who she'd met at the textile mill where she'd worked in Danville. They were both in the bowling league for the mill. He was crazy about her. She liked him a lot and her mother approved of him, which was important to her. One Saturday night they went to a local drive-in to see the movie, *The Goodbye Girl*. They both loved the movie. It had an 'opposite attracts' theme and was quite funny. Her favorite actor was Richard Dreyfuss and he was very good in it. Afterwards, they went up to a popular spot where couples went to make out and more… Things got out of control and she gave up her virginity. She was not sorry she did it, though, and Ben had a condom on him. He told her all men carried one in their wallet. It was a 'coming of age' sign, he'd explained. But she could tell he was not a novice. It was a little clumsy doing it in the back seat but they were both on the short side so it wasn't too difficult. She continued to date Ben and they even got a motel room a few times. But when the mill closed, Anna wanted to go to school in Syracuse, and their relationship ended. *You never forget your first*, she mused.

They moved to the bedroom. Moe was curled up on the bed but quickly jumped down when they plopped down on it. Max was a skillful lover. She could tell right away by the way he moved up and down her body. Before she knew it, she was completely naked and he was removing his clothes as quickly as possible. He'd pulled a condom out of his wallet. Afterwards, they cuddled and Max spent the night.

They both had to get up and get to work in the morning. Max did not have his uniform, of course, so he left at four-forty to get home so he could be at work by six o'clock. Anna basked in the glow for a while longer. She knew she was falling in love with Max and thought he felt the same. She knew she had satisfied him sexually. She finally got up and showered and dressed. She fed Moe and apologized for displacing him last evening, but he did not seem bothered by it.

She drove her car to work for the first time. *What a time saver!* she thought. No buses to catch or transfers to make. She was grateful. She'd call an insurance company during her lunchtime and would also run to the bank around the corner from work to transfer the money. She would have a busy day but was glad for it.

Max decided to stop going to the bar. He was falling in love with Anna. He wanted to take her home to meet his mother and family and he was eager to meet her family as well. He decided he'd stop at her place after she got home today.

He got there at six-fifteen and was relieved that she was glad to see him. She said she'd transferred the money for the car and called the seller to tell her the check would be good by Thursday. She'd also already gotten insurance. "It all just fell into place," she said happily. "Except I didn't have time for lunch," she laughed.

Max said, "I'm amazed at what you can accomplish, Anna," then gave her a light kiss on the lips and a pat on her rear end.

Chapter - 45

The first Saturday in October, Anna brought Max home to Danville. Her mother greeted them at the door and was very cordial to Max. She had met him when he helped Anna move but only briefly. Anna's sister, Audrey, and her husband Dale had come over for lunch and her brother, Hugh, would come by after he finished his shift at Walmart. Her mom subtly grilled Max about his background. Two weekends earlier, Max had taken Anna to meet his mother in Oneida. His father had died two years earlier at one of his local watering holes. He'd been a heavy drinker, but the cause of death was listed as heart attack. Mrs. Strickland greeted Anna warmly and they had a lovely afternoon getting to know one another. Most of Max's siblings had moved out of state, but the two sisters who lived nearby dropped in together to see Max and meet Anna. Anna was pleased to discover that she liked all of them.

They got home late that night and Max stayed over, especially since they could sleep in the next day. Before they made love, they discussed their families and what they liked and did not like. Max thought Anna's brother-in-law, Dale, was a little too 'uppity,' as he called it. "I just thought he was a little full of himself, that's all," said Max. Anna wondered if he was jealous that Dale had a profession and was in line for the family business. She let it go, though, and had nothing negative to say about his family.

"I thought your mother and sisters were all very sweet. I hope to get some parenting tips from your mom," she looked up at him flirtatiously.

"Let's get practicing, how about it?" asked Max as he wrapped his arms around her and started undoing the buttons on her pretty pink blouse.

"Yes, let's," grinned Anna.

Six weeks later, Anna found out she was pregnant. She suspected when she missed her period but hoped it was just from stress. They'd had sex when they got home from her mother's and when Max was finished he removed the condom and noticed a tear in it when he went to flush it. He almost didn't say anything but decided honesty was warranted, especially in this case. They had been talking about marriage and Max was spending the night at her place more and more often. He'd even left two of his uniforms at her place for when he spent the night on a weeknight.

They arranged a quick marriage at the Justice of the Peace the weekend before Thanksgiving. They had no one to join them as witnesses, so the judge called on his staff members. They called their families on Thanksgiving Day to share the news and their mothers were a bit shocked and disappointed at being deprived of a wedding, but nevertheless said they were happy for them. Anna's coworkers threw together a lovely wedding shower for her in December. Barbara, the woman she'd befriended on her second day and often ate lunch with, held it at her apartment not far from work. Anna received many gifts, including a beautiful and very revealing lingerie set. Everyone got a kick out of it. Anna had not yet told anyone she was pregnant. She was superstitious about telling people in the first trimester so she decided to wait until after the new year.

Max helped her bring all the gifts up to the apartment. A friend had helped him move his furniture to Anna's apartment the previous week. Since they only had a one bedroom and Anna had a bedroom set, he decided to rent a storage unit where he could keep his. He was thinking ahead about when they had children. He gave away his sofa and living room furniture, but brought over the second-hand dining table and chairs that his sister had given him when he'd moved out. Anna wasn't crazy about the dark color but just said she would paint it after the baby was born.

As Anna wrote her thank you notes the following week for her shower gifts, Max went out Christmas shopping. He came home with a small tree and some trim. It was artificial, but it was very attractive and they enjoyed decorating it together.

Anna was over the moon. She had a job that paid well, with a path to advancement and now a husband she loved and a baby on the way, who was going to be very lucky. She could not imagine being any more in love or happier.

Caroline Ruth Strickland was born on July 2, 1982. She weighed 7 lbs., 1 oz, and was 18 and 1/2 inches long. She was perfect. Anna had had a normal pregnancy and the delivery was relatively easy. She was exuberant after the birth and ready to go home. A nurse from the La Leche League, an organization that helped educate new mothers on breastfeeding, had come and shown her how easy it was to breastfeed Caroline, who turned out to be very easy to satisfy. She just nursed and slept, all day long. They went home the next day. Max's mother had bought them a car seat that turned into a carrier. Her mother had bought them a crib. Max had set up the nursery in the corner of their bedroom. It was cramped but they weren't ready to move just yet. They'd heard a two-bedroom apartment would be available in the building in a couple of months, and they wanted to wait because they really liked the building and location.

Anna had six paid weeks of leave and Max took a week of vacation. They settled into a routine. Anna started pumping her milk pretty quickly and planned to freeze it for when she went back to work. Fortunately, there was a woman in their building who keeps only infants in her apartment. Anna managed to snag a spot with her starting at the end of August. She also had some vacation coming, so thought she might even take an extra week of maternity leave. If they had more children, Anna hoped she might be able to become a stay-at-home mom, but for now, they needed her income.

Once Max went back to work, Anna had to manage on her own. Her mother offered to come and stay a week but Anna told her she would be okay. She was strong and wanted to manage her home the way she wanted it. Time management was the key, she knew. Caroline nursed every two to three hours so it was hard to plan to go out to do anything, but the weather was so nice she decided to take her down to the nearby park in her stroller, which her co-workers had all gone in on together. She met a couple of other mothers who lived in the neighborhood so she was happy to make some friends. It was so easy to get bored with no one around but a sleeping infant. The mothers told her they met in the park every afternoon around 3:00 because that seemed to be between feedings and before dinner. She was thrilled and thought it worked perfectly with her own schedule.

That night she told Max about meeting the other mothers and their routine. He was happy for her and agreed that she and Caroline both needed to get out and get fresh air. "It'll be cold before we know it."

At her six week mark, her doctor cleared her for sexual intercourse, so she and Max made up for several weeks of abstinence in one night. Fortunately, Caroline cooperated and slept through their noisy sex acts. Max, of course, enjoyed the new size of her breasts but after a while she had to pump, so Max cradled Caroline while Anna pumped her milk.

Chapter - 46

By November, Max and Anna had moved into a two-bedroom in the building, so Caroline had her own nursery. Anna had painted it pink and decorated it from the JCPenney's catalog. She'd received a promotion shortly after returning to work and was now supervisor of the entire data entry department. She was responsible for hiring, firing, reviews, production and reports - many, many reports. It seemed all she did was write and create reports. But she was happy to be doing something different. She was well-liked by her co-workers and did not anticipate too many headaches. The company paid well and employee retention was important to their bottom line. Her new salary helped with the higher rent they were now paying, as well as the cost of babysitting.

Max had been with the bus company for about six years but there were few opportunities for advancement with the transit company, because once someone was given a supervisory role, they usually stayed until they retired. There was very little employee turnover. The only financial saving grace was that he received an automatic cost of living increase every year. He'd stopped going to the bar when he decided he was going to marry Anna. He was dedicated to being a good husband and father. He went home gladly at three o'clock every day and most days he picked up Caroline from the babysitter so Anna could come right home and they could make dinner together.

Their lives continued on like this for another three and a half years, until Anna got pregnant again. She was thrilled. She and Max went together to view the ultrasound, to find out if it was a boy or a girl. She had a feeling that Max wanted a boy, but the ultrasound determined that they were having another girl. Max seemed happy and said, "The baby's healthy and that's what counts." Anna was relieved he felt that way and loved him for it.

The next day after Max got off work, he went to the bar. It was the biggest mistake he would ever make. It led to him returning to the bar several times a week. He did his best to hide it from Anna but she was becoming suspicious. One night she came home and the apartment was empty. She went to the babysitters, where she found Caroline waiting to be picked up. Mrs. Harper suggested that now Caroline was potty trained, they might want to start looking for a nursery to take her. "I really only take care of infants," she said apologetically. "But I can give you some names of places to check out."

"Oh, I'm sorry, I guess I hadn't thought far enough ahead. I've actually just found out I'm pregnant again and due in about seven months. I'll start looking for a nursery school for Caroline, but do you think you'll be available when the baby comes?" asked Anna hopefully.

Mrs. Harper looked closely at Anna and paused. She took a breath and said as kindly as she could, "I have to tell you, Anna dear, your husband has come to get Caroline a few times and I could smell the alcohol on his breath."

Anna stared at her in shock, then said, "There must be some mistake, Mrs. Harper. Max doesn't drink."

"Oh honey, I know you probably believe that, but I lived with an alcoholic at one time, and I can smell it a mile away."

Anna didn't know how to respond so simply gathered Caroline and thanked her. Once she had Caroline settled in her highchair for her dinner, Anna began thinking about the times she'd come home and Max had been a little more animated and louder than usual. She could even smell mouthwash on his breath. She started shaking uncontrollably and then began crying.

Max walked in a few minutes later and saw how distraught Anna was. He asked her if something had happened at work and she just shook her head and glared at him. Finally, she blurted out, "Mrs. Harper said we need to look for a nursery school for Caroline since she's potty-trained now and I told her we were having another baby and wondered if she would be willing to babysit when the time comes."

Max looked confused and said, "Okaaay…great. So what did she say?"

"I'll tell you what she said," Anna raised her voice, which was incredibly uncharacteristic of her. "She smelled alcohol on your breath a couple of times when you picked Caroline up. Please explain to me why you would go drinking and then pick our daughter up!"

Max just looked down at his feet and said, "I'm sorry, Anna, I should never have done that." He turned and went into their bedroom and laid down.

Anna followed him and asked again, "Why would you go to a bar? Are you not happy being here with me and Caroline?"

Max said he didn't know why he'd done it, it had only been a couple of times, he said of course he was happy, and promised to never do it again. Anna believed him because in her heart she knew he loved her and Caroline, but also because what choice did she have?

Chapter - 47

As far as Anna knew Max never left work and went to the bar again. They would occasionally go out to dinner and he would have a beer, but it did not seem to be an ongoing problem. She prayed every night that their marriage was solid and both of them cared enough about each other and their growing family.

On May 4, 1986, Elizabeth Monica Strickland was born. She was 8 lbs. 4 oz. and Anna required a cesarean section. She was such a chubby little baby with a headful of beautiful black hair. The hair would almost all fall out within a month but it was nice while she had it. They named her Elizabeth after Max's mother and his oldest sister, but Max preferred to call her by her middle name of Monica.

Their two bedroom apartment was getting crowded. By the time Monica was born, Anna had arranged for Caroline to attend a preschool near where she worked. It was called Little Tykes and Mrs. Harper had recommended it. They also had a nursery, so Anna decided it was more convenient and made the most sense to put both girls there. She had received several raises over the years, and was established in her job, and Max was hitting his ten year mark with the transit authority so would be making more money. They decided to start looking for a home.

Anna had taken a real estate course, thinking she might go into real estate sales before Monica was born but was mostly trying to educate herself on the process of buying a house. She knew Max didn't know much about it and he was not as adept with finances as she was. She met with her banker and found out how much they could be pre-approved for, based on their combined incomes. Between her and Max's bonuses, she'd been able to save a sizable amount for a down payment over the last five years. Other than visiting family, they had not taken a vacation since they were married. She was more interested in providing for her family than laying on a beach.

They were approved for an amount that would get them a three bedroom in the suburbs, so she went to a real estate agent named Andrew Baker, who'd been recommended by her friend and co-worker Barbara. He gave them his speech about what he'd do for them if they chose him as their agent and they agreed to move forward with the search. Andrew set up four showings for them very quickly, all in areas with good schools. The following Saturday, Mrs. Harper was thankfully free to watch Caroline and Monica so Max and Anna could see some homes.

They spent the morning touring all four houses, but were not satisfied. Andrew sensed their disappointment and after they stopped at McDonald's for lunch, he told them he had a couple more he wanted to show them. He said they both needed a little work and wasn't sure how handy they were after living in an apartment for so long, but he thought they might want to see them anyway.

Anna said, "We don't mind doing our own work. My brother, Hugh, is a carpenter and my brother-in-law Dale is a plumber. He owns his own company," she added.

Max agreed. He was eager to work on his own place. He told Andrew he had watched his father fix many things in their house while growing up. "I think we could handle it," he winked at Anna.

They looked at two fixer-uppers and were finally excited by one of them, making their offer that afternoon when they returned home. They offered $5,000 under the asking price. Andrew promised to contact the selling agent and get back to them as soon as possible. Anna and Max were on pins and needles. It seemed they both really wanted the house. It was very cute and had great curb appeal, as well as a fenced-in backyard. There really was not a lot of "fixing up" beyond painting and a bit of elbow grease. It had been built in the early 1970's and had carpeting throughout, along with dark cabinetry, which Anna was eager to change out, but it was in good condition overall.

The seller countered with $3,000 under their asking, which only raised Anna and Max's offer by $2,000, and Andrew advised them he thought it was a good and fair offer, so they agreed. Suddenly they were homeowners and there was a lot to do. They immediately gave their notice to the superintendent that they would be moving. The closing would be in forty-five days, after all the standard protocols were conducted. They would be patient, as they had plenty to do to prepare.

Anna arranged a moving van for the weekend after closing. No one was living in the home so there was no issue with when they could get in. On closing day, they got the keys and immediately took the children to the house. They were so excited. They ended up ordering a pizza to take back to their apartment. The following Saturday morning, the moving van arrived. Anna and Max had been packing for two weeks and had loaded both of their cars with things they knew they'd need right away. Monica was still under six months old so there was a lot she needed. Anna's mother drove over to help with the children while they moved in. She offered to take them back home with her but Anna gently refused the offer. She always wanted her children with her, but especially now.

That afternoon they finished cleaning the apartment and completed the check sheet. There wasn't much damage considering how long they'd lived there, so they thought there would be no question about getting their deposit back. The superintendent said they didn't need to worry about the carpets because their unit would be painted and re-carpeted anyway. He wished them well when they turned in the key and told them he would miss seeing the children. Anna promised to come by sometime when she was in town. They had already bid Mrs. Harper goodbye the day before and the lovely woman had given each of the girls a music box for their bedrooms.

They drove back to their new house, where Ruth, Anna's mother was watching the girls. On the way they picked up a bucket of fried chicken. Anna's mother had already gotten Monica's bedding on her crib and was feeding her in the kitchen. They all decided that since it was late and it was a two hour drive home, she should spend the night on the sofa.

It had been a long day and everyone was ready to turn in. Anna and Max put their bedframe together and found fresh sheets, as well as a blanket and pillow for her mother. The next morning, Ruth kissed them all and said goodbye. She told Anna she was proud of her and thought the house they'd chosen was lovely. Anna thanked her mother and promised to visit with the girls very soon.

Part - 4

Chapter - 48

January 1, 1990

Max and Anna threw a New Year's Eve party. They had been in their home for just over three years and had never thrown a party before. They invited friends from work and a few neighbors. Anna had driven seven year-old Caroline and three year-old Monica to her mother's two days ago. They'd celebrated this Christmas with Max's family. They alternated families between Thanksgiving and Christmas every year.

Ruth was happy to see the children but thought Anna looked distraught. "Are you okay, sweetie?" she asked.

"I'm fine, Mom. Just tired from party planning. And of course, the trip to Oneida and all the wrapping of presents and everything. I'll be fine in a few days. I took two weeks off from work so I have another week to rest up."

"Okay, honey, but you know I worry about my children. It's called being a mother."

Anna said she knew the feeling well. What she didn't say was that she and Max had been having marital problems lately. Starting in October, Max had been getting home from work later and later. She knew he liked to stop by and see his friends at the bar from time to time and she did not begrudge him that but his moods seemed to be shifting. *A mid-life crisis?* she wondered. But Max was only thirty-six. Their sex life was as good as it always was. She didn't think he was having an affair but she confronted him anyway and he hit the roof.

"Of course not!" he screamed. "When would I even have time?"

She dropped it because she had no proof and didn't want to make more trouble. That was why she'd suggested having the New Year's Eve party - to get them back on track with each other. He was involved in all of the planning and didn't question her about anything. They invited twelve couples between them and she invited her friend Barbara, who was still single, and Max invited his friend from the bar, Roy.

They asked their guests to bring an appetizer and BYOB. They provided the mixers and Max made pulled pork. Anna made a chocolate cake and bought some pies at the local bakery. Everyone seemed to enjoy the food and complimented Anna on her decorating of the house. They played music and people danced around the living room. At midnight, the TV was tuned to Times Square and they all sung *Auld Lang Syne* and kissed.

By the time everyone had left, it was two-thirty. Max and Anna decided to clean up in the morning because they were ready to drop. The next morning, they slept late. Anna finally got up and made coffee and let Max sleep a bit longer. She reflected on the evening. Everyone had behaved themselves, meaning, as far as she knew, no one had over-indulged. Barbara and Roy seemed to get on well and everyone had mingled nicely. Suddenly, Max called out, "Woman, get in here to bed!" She laughed and walked in doing a little stripper dance. They made love and she thought everything was right with the world. It had been a long time since she'd felt that way. Too long.

Anna has been on the pill for a while. She'd tried an IUD but she had stomach cramps so her gynecologist took her off of it. She said to Max, "If we're through making babies, I could have my tubes tied or you could get a vasectomy."

He winced at the thought. She punched his shoulder and told him he was a chicken. They would have to make a decision sometime soon.

"Why don't we try for a boy?" suggested Max.

"We can think about it but I'd want to stop working and stay home."

Anna felt like she was doing everything around the house plus making dinner every night. She wondered why Max would not help her like he used to. He seemed to be getting lazy. She also noticed he was stopping to have a beer at the bar a little more often than usual. She hated to be a nagging wife but she simply did not understand why he had to go to the bar. There was plenty to do at home and she would've appreciated him coming home to help, even if it just meant doing a load of laundry or emptying the dishwasher. She was seriously considering hiring a cleaning person if this kept up.

One night in early April, Max came home more inebriated than she had ever seen him. She could not believe he had driven home in that condition. If he were ever to get a DUI, he would be automatically fired from his job.

She said, "You seem more drunk than usual, what's going on with you?"

He instantly became irate and struck her so hard on her right shoulder that it knocked her to the floor. He immediately reached out to help her up but she pushed him away and told him to leave her alone.

Thankfully, the girls were already in bed so they never knew what happened. Max was very upset and apologized profusely. He promised her over and over that it would never happen again. He said, "I just don't know what came over me, Anna. Please, honey, can you forgive me?"

Anna had believed in forgiveness all her life, having been raised a Christian. But she wasn't sure she could forget. She got up and went to the sink to get a drink of water. Then she turned to Max and said, "I'm going to bed. I don't want to talk to you tonight."

Max stayed up late that night. He had a headache from the beer he'd been drinking on an empty stomach so he took some aspirin and drank a Pepsi. It seemed to take the edge off. Then he realized how thirsty he was and drank a whole glass of ice water. He swore to himself that he would never hurt his wife and would stop drinking. He remembered having nightmares as a child of his father coming home drunk and could hear his parents fighting. As far as he knew, his father had never hit his mother, though, and this thought alone scared him witless. *Is there something wrong with me that I would hit a woman, let alone my own wife?* he wondered.

Chapter - 49

That same year, Max and Anna decided to surprise the girls for their birthdays by taking them on a real family vacation, a Disney Cruise, so Anna went to a travel agency near work and booked it. They would fly to Orlando on July 27th and stay in a resort at Disney World the night before the cruise. Both girls had parties on their actual birthdays - Monica on May 4th and Caroline on July 2nd - where they received Disney-related gifts that they were very satisfied with. Anna was pleased to see that they seemed to have no idea about the upcoming cruise.

Max had not come home late since the incident in April. Anna had forgiven him and understood he was under a lot of pressure, just as she was with taking care of the home and the children. They discussed having another child and Anna went off birth control.

Max brought home a Tinkerbell nightlight for the girls' room the day before they left and plugged it in when they went to bed. He and Anna tucked them in and told them they were leaving the next day. The girls could barely sleep. Anna had already packed for them, so the next day they flew to Orlando and stayed in the resort that night. The girls were over the moon with excitement.

They arrived at the hotel late in the afternoon, and were all tired from the flight. Max went out and found a taco place nearby and brought back dinner to eat in their rooms. The next morning, they were shuttled to the boat loading area and were directed to a staging area where they waited for what seemed a long time to board. When it was finally their turn, they first took pictures with Mickey and Minnie before going to their cabin. It was a beautiful cabin and fairly large, with a queen bed for Anna and Max and bunk beds for the girls. Three-year-old Monica got the bottom bunk, of course, which was fine with Caroline, who wanted to be on top.

There were activities every day. The girls had a tea party with Cinderella on Tuesday. Anna had packed their prettiest dresses just for that occasion. The rest of the time they mostly stayed in their swimsuits. One day was set aside for parents to have time to themselves. The girls and other children were watched over by Goofy in a playground on the upper deck. Anna checked it out carefully before she left them there but it was well-secured. They'd be there for four hours or until parents came to get them.

Anna and Max made good use of their private time. They stopped at the parents' bar room and had a drink, then headed to their cabin to try to make a baby. She'd read somewhere that to make a boy you had to be on top, but even if that was a myth, it was fine because she really enjoyed that position. They had two sessions in the bed and when it got close to the time to pick up the girls, they made love again in the teeny shower. It was clumsier than Anna's first time in the back seat of Ben's car, but she had no real complaints.

They picked up the girls, who regaled them with stories about their fun day. The next few days flew by. Late one night, after the girls were sound asleep, Max was very amorous and rolled Anna over and climbed on top. She was still mostly asleep but she woke up and easily accepted him. She often wondered if this was when their baby boy was conceived.

The week flew by and before they knew it, it was Saturday morning, their last day. As they waited at the airport for their return flight, Max took the girls for ice cream and let Anna have some time for herself. She wandered the airport and at the Hudson gift shop, she saw a newspaper with a headline about a girl who lived near Syracuse having disappeared. She'd been at a party and walking home alone at night when she went missing. Apparently, she was the second girl who'd gone missing in the last year. There was speculation that there could be a serial killer loose in the area. It really opened Anna's eyes about the predators out there. As a mother with two little girls that she would do anything to protect, it frightened her.

Max and the girls caught up with her and they boarded their flight. The girls slept the entire trip. They were home by seven. Anna made the girls each a sandwich for dinner and got them to bed. Their vet had a boarding service where clients could leave their pets while they were out of town, so Anna would pick Moe up in the morning. All in all, Anna thought everything was in order. She and Max were both very glad they'd taken this vacation with their girls. They had a lot of pictures to develop and Anna planned to make a little album for each of the girls, as well as a family album. As she drifted off to sleep that night, she thought happily about the baby she just might be carrying.

Chapter - 50

Anna knew she was pregnant. Two weeks after returning to work from vacation she simply sensed it. But she waited four weeks, then purchased a pregnancy test from the drugstore, and it was positive. Max was delighted and couldn't wait to see the ultrasound. Anna had more morning sickness from this pregnancy than from the previous two, and believed this to be a sign she was carrying a boy.

Max still wanted to have sex and she complied, but only once, because this pregnancy felt different and she was afraid of losing the baby. She went to her doctor at eight weeks to verify the pregnancy and heard the heartbeat. The doctor told her everything looked good and she should come back in four weeks, but she wanted to wait until the fourth month before doing an ultrasound. "If you want to know if it's a boy, it would be easier to tell by then," said her doctor.

Max was getting restless, though. He wanted to know if he could look forward to a boy, and he also wanted to have sex. Back in April, when he'd slipped with the drinking, there'd also been one indiscretion he was not proud of, but now he was itching to do it again. Anna would never know. The girl was merely a one night floozy, after all. It was a woman who worked at the station where he checked in. Her name was Honey, and that she was.

Anna had been very strict about no sex until after the ultrasound, which would be at least another month. One afternoon after Max had clocked out, Honey was walking in from a break. She worked in the back office doing payroll. He asked her about one of his paychecks, saying he thought he had overtime but had not been paid. They both knew it was a ruse, but she led him to the back office anyway. There were blinds on the office windows that she kept closed at all times for privacy. As soon as the door was closed, she locked it and unzipped his pants for him. The next twenty minutes was heaven on earth for Max. He was glad Honey was on the pill but he had a condom on him anyway, for STD protection. Honey always wore skirts for a reason and their quickie was over before he knew it. He left work with a smile on his face and a spring in his step. He would be home on time and have a load of laundry done and put away before Anna arrived home with the girls.

Anna had an ultrasound after Thanksgiving, and it was clearly a boy. Max was beaming and went out and bought blue fake cigars to be ready. Anna was very pleased and called her family that evening. She felt good because the doctor had said the fetus looked perfect. Her family was very happy for her. Max called his mother and two of his sisters and asked them to share the good news with the rest of the family. The due date was April 15th but since Anna had a cesarean with Monica, the doctor said they might need to do another cesarean, in which case it could be earlier. It would depend on how large the baby is in the last month.

That night they made love with Anna on top, since that had become her favorite and most satisfying position. Max didn't mind one way or the other, as long as he got sex again. They 'spooned' for a while afterwards and talked about what color to paint the nursery, blue or green? They couldn't decide. Then their discussion became more serious. Anna wanted to stay home with the children. It would be more cost effective in the long run than more babysitters and daycare. Max agreed. He had grown up with a mom at home and felt Anna needed that chance to be a full-time mom. They had been careful with their money, thanks to Anna saving every chance she got. He was a lucky man, he thought as he drifted off to sleep. The next morning, he woke up to Anna in the bathroom vomiting. He was worried about her but she assured him it would stop soon.

Christmas 1990 arrived. They tried to pare back on buying

presents because they had to plan for just one paycheck after the baby came. They'd decided on a name based on each of their fathers: Joseph Edward. Joseph for Anna's father and Edward for Max's. They both immediately agreed to call him Joey, though, because they thought that was a great name for a little boy. He would probably become Joe as he got older. Anna was not up to traveling that year so her mother came over on Christmas day and helped Anna prepare a wonderful meal for her whole family. The following weekend Max's mother drove over with her daughter, Elizabeth, to help with the meal, and Max's family came for a belated Christmas dinner. They decided to have a quiet evening at home for New Year's Eve, especially since Anna was five months pregnant by then and even though the morning sickness had subsided, she still didn't have the energy she'd had when she was pregnant with the girls.

The following week, Anna was back at work and Max had picked up a different route. Drivers were being moved around so he would not be seeing Honey again, which was fine with him. He knew he had to straighten up and become the real man of the family, and he wanted to do that for his children, but especially for Anna. She worked so hard, and was always sacrificing for her family.

In February they finally picked out a light blue color for the nursery, and bought a nice bumper pad and matching sheets with blue and green balloons. Max found a picture of Babe Ruth and sneaked it into the nursery and hung it before Anna saw it. She laughed and said, "You'll be the one coaching him, so have fun."

Chapter - 51

Joseph "Joey" Edward Strickland was born by cesarean section on April 5, 1991. He weighed in at 8 lbs., was 22" in length and was a big boy from the start. Anna nursed him like a pro. She was able to leave the hospital in three days and the girls were very sweet with their little brother. He was their pride and joy. Anna was more relaxed with her third baby. She had resigned her job, giving her company thirty days' notice, as was the practice for anyone in management. Her friend Barbara was promoted to her job and Anna enjoyed training her because it was such a breeze. They spent more time just talking about life than about work. Barbara was in a relationship with a man she'd met at church. There were no plans of marriage yet but she didn't rule it out.

Anna got into a routine of taking Joey for a walk in his stroller most days, and had taken Monica out of daycare so she could spend the days with her mother as well. She would be starting kindergarten in the fall, so Anna wanted to enjoy having her with her all day until then. Once in a while she would load them in the car and take them to the local park. She usually did the grocery shopping on the weekend because it was too much during the week with both Joey and Monica, so she would get up early on Saturday to do it. Max would wake the kids and make their breakfast on Saturday, and give Joey a bottle when Anna was out.

Everything was going great… until it wasn't.

Max came home on a Friday in June and told Anna the transit

system had been sold to a large conglomerate and he was being laid off. His last day would be June 29th. He had been there over twelve years. He had been a good employee with nothing negative in his personnel file. He rarely called in sick and was never late. He was in a state of shock. They gave him twelve weeks of pay and he would be able to collect unemployment. Anna didn't know what to say. She was devastated and worried. How would they pay for their medical insurance? Max would have no benefits now.

Max became depressed. He didn't know how to act without a job. He knew Anna was upset. She didn't deserve this after leaving a good-paying job to be a stay-at-home mom. He bought a bottle of tequila and told himself he would just drink a shot every now and then to take the edge off. The girls were getting on his nerves and Joey seemed to always be crying. He wondered how Anna did it all day. He worked in the yard more than usual but that didn't help his mood.

Anna suggested he go to Mass. Maybe re-connecting with his religious upbringing would help him, but he had no idea how to do that. He'd never gone to Mass as an adult, except at Christmas and Easter. He started to hit the bottle more often.

One night he told Anna he wanted to go to the bar and catch up with some of his friends. She told him to go. She thought it might help get some of the depression out of his system. Meanwhile she was trying to figure out what Max could do for a living. He didn't have a college degree or trade school education and driving a bus was all he had ever done.

He spent several hours at the bar. In fact, he had to come home in a taxi because he knew he was too inebriated to drive. Anna helped him into bed and went back to sleep but woke up suddenly and found him not beside her. She got up and found him in the living room watching TV.

"How do you feel?" Anna asked him.

"Thirsty," he replied.

She went into the kitchen to get him a glass of water. When she gave it to him she sat down next to him and asked him what was wrong. He said he just did not know what to do to besides drive a transit bus. He told her he was too old to learn anything new and was deflated.

Anna was very tender and took his hand and led him back to bed. Once they got settled she tried to be romantic, hoping he would know she understood and loved him. But he rolled over and got as far away from her in the bed as he could. She was scared she was losing him.

The next morning Anna made breakfast and set the table like it was a special morning. Max finally got out of bed and came to the table. By then the children had eaten and were watching TV. She needed to nurse Joey so she was rushing to get Max's food ready for him. She had just poured him a cup of coffee when she said to him that she had an idea of what he could do. "I think you should look into becoming a long distance truck driver, Max, it is what you love to do and I hear they make great money."

Max looked at her and frowned as he said, "Is that all I am to you, a paycheck?"

Anna did not know what to say. It was so out of character for Max to behave like this. He laid on the sofa watching mindless TV for the rest of the day. It had been three weeks since he'd been laid off. Sure, they had income coming in, but she knew how fast that would disappear with three kids. Unemployment would definitely not cover their bills and she was getting nervous. Since it was a beautiful summer day, she put the children in the car and took them to the park. In the car, she asked Caroline if she was ok. Caroline had bad dreams sometimes and could be sleepy and cranky, so she asked her if she had a bad dream last night. Caroline told her no, she didn't remember it.

Monica was quiet. Anna wasn't sure what to think about this. She suddenly remembered a vet appointment for Moe that afternoon so she had to get the children home to have Max watch them, but when they got home, Max wasn't there. Where could he have gone? She'd forgotten to tell him about the appointment but he must have seen it on the calendar she kept on the refrigerator. She had to get Moe into his carrier and get to the vet with all three kids. Luckily Caroline was old enough to be a big help and carried Moe.

Max was still gone when they got home. Anna fed and bathed

Joey and got him to sleep, then helped Caroline and Monica get their baths.

Anna was sitting in the living room when Max came through the kitchen door, trying to be quiet, but doing it very poorly. He bumped into the kitchen table. Anna thought one of the children would wake up but they didn't. She rose slowly and walked into the kitchen and just stood in the doorway. Max looked at her and said, "What?" a little too aggressively.

"What", repeated Anna. "You disappeared this afternoon, Max. I had to load up the children to take Moe to the vet. Why are you behaving like a child?"

Max lunged and grabbed her by the neck and bent her over so far backward, she felt her lower back almost crack. She thought he was going to choke her to death. Then he just threw her to the floor. He stomped out the back door and got in the car and left. He did not return for three days.

Anna had had enough and she called the police and when they came to the house, she told them what her husband had done and showed them the reddened area around her neck and the bruise on her knee and her elbow from him throwing her to the floor. They took the report and asked if she wanted to go to the hospital to get checked out, but she refused because she had no one to watch the children. Then they wanted to know if she would press charges against him. They explained he would be arrested when they found him and would be arraigned which meant a night at least in jail and he would go before the judge. There more than likely would be a fine and no jail time but probation. "You could also take out a restraining order," the officer told her.

Anna had to weigh everything and could not imagine putting her children through the shame of having their father thrown in jail. "Will you keep the report on file, if I don't file charges right now?"

The officers told her it would be recorded as a domestic act call and if it happens again it can be used against him. That satisfied Anna. At least there is a record. The officer took pictures of her neck and the bruises on her elbow and knee. "You should put something on that elbow, it appears the skin was broken." Anna told him thank you and she will take care of it after they leave.

"Is there anything else we can do for you today, ma'am?"

"No, you have been a big help and have explained my options. Thank you."

They left after that, wishing her well and told her to call anytime she felt threatened.

She went to check on the children. She knew Joey was in the bed asleep but she wondered if Monica and Caroline would have heard the policemen.

The girls were in Caroline's room and they were listening to songs on the tape player she had received for Christmas. They were careful about the music the girls listened to and Anna was happy to see they were singing along to an older tape of the New Kids on the Block. The music was loud and she does not think they heard anything. She told them to turn it down some so Joey would not wake up.

Chapter - 52

When Max returned, he told her he'd applied for a job with Walmart. The job was pending approval for his commercial driver's license. He would be a long-haul trucker up and down the East Coast and would probably start by the end of August. He said he'd be very careful with the budget until then but she should not buy anything extra until he was fully employed. She told him that Caroline and Monica needed school clothes, so he gave her a small budget and told her to start looking at Goodwill stores. In fact, he told her to shop there for whatever she needed until he said otherwise. He said since he was the only one working now, he would call the shots.

Anna was beside herself, not knowing why Max had changed so very much. She tried to hold it together for the sake of the children. Max went to the bar every night and came home late. He expected sex whenever he wanted it, no matter how she felt about it. She had never seen this side of him and it scared her. One day she begged him to go to counseling together but he said he didn't need any damn counseling. She told him they obviously had different views and if he didn't want to go, she'd at least go on her own. He was sullen and angry at her for the rest of the day.

That night, she heard him get up and go to the bathroom. She fell back asleep but awakened with a start a little while later. She just laid there for a while, listening to the house settling in the middle of the night.

She almost got up to see if he had left but she waited. When Max came back to bed, she pretended to be asleep. But she could not sleep for the rest of the night. That night she decided she would have to get away from her husband, not only for her own sake but for her children's' sake, as well.

The next day, she took the girls to the playground and left Joey at home with Max. She asked Monica if she had been ill or had a nightmare last night.

Monica shook her head and said, "Daddy came in to say good night and stayed with me until I went to sleep."

"That's all?" asked Anna, not knowing what she wanted to hear.

"Yes, Mommy," nodded Monica. Anna wasn't sure what to make of any of this anymore. Was she being paranoid? All Monica would say was that he'd helped her get to sleep. She prayed that was all there was to it.

When they got home, Monica went to her room and stayed there. It was not like her. Max was in the family room watching TV, as usual. It was August 25th and he hadn't received his license yet. Anna started to wonder whether he had even applied. She felt like she was mentally losing it. She went to check on Monica and found her curled up on her bed, so she sat down beside her and asked her what was wrong.

Monica said she felt bad because she thought maybe she was making Anna mad at Daddy.

"Why would you say that?" asked Anna, mystified.

"Because you don't talk to him like you used to."

Anna knew she needed to be careful with her next words. "Sweetheart, sometimes moms and dads just have a rough patch of not getting along. Daddy is going through a hard time and I am trying to understand it." Monica said, "okay," and just put her head under the pillow.

Anna went into the family room and found Max again in front of the TV.

She asked him what she had done wrong in their marriage and why he was acting the way he was acting. She told him she cannot let him abuse her the way he had been doing or she would leave him. He stood up and went over to her and slapped her across the face so hard it stung. He said "Don't ever tell me what I can and cannot do in my own house. You have been in charge for too long and now it is my turn. He just walked out the door and did not come back. The next day, Max had not returned and she was beside herself. This was the breaking point. She did not know any of his friends except Roy, but did not know him well. She was concerned about her children and their welfare. What if he has left for good? The children would want to know, so she just told them he went to check on their grandmother who had been taken to the hospital.

Chapter - 53

Max

Max had just returned from his first run up and down the East Coast. He walked in the house and found it empty except for Moe, who was meowing and walking between his legs every chance he got. He wondered why Moe was being so loving toward him. He checked the laundry room where his food and water were and noticed the continuous water and food containers were out. His litter box was clean. He called out but got no answer. He looking around for a note or some indication about where Anna and the kids might be. He wished he'd called yesterday from the road. When he left two weeks ago, they were not on speaking terms. He'd been hard on Anna about the budget and told her to start going to Goodwill to look for clothes for the children. She blamed him for their marital troubles just because he was trying to take some authority. She had been in charge their entire marriage and now that she had quit her job to stay home, he was supposed to be the breadwinner but he was not doing a very good job of it. He had not yet received his driving license for the eighteen wheeler he was expected to be able to manage. He was worried that he had not passed the driving skill test but he didn't want to tell Anna this because she was so good at everything. When she came and told him she would leave him if things did not change, he was so angry, he'd slapped her, then left and stayed at Tammy's, his old girlfriend from the bar.

A couple of days later he found out he'd been approved for his commercial driver's license and they wanted to put him on the road right away. He went home and found the house empty. He guessed Anna had just gone out shopping with the kids. He'd gathered some clothes and toiletries for the road and left her a note saying that he was leaving on his first run and would be in touch in a few days. Unfortunately, he hadn't followed through and hadn't called her the entire time he was gone.

He waited the rest of the day, thinking they'd be home any time. He had done a lot of thinking while he was on his trip and knew he had to change his ways if he hoped to keep Anna and his kids happy. He worried he was becoming his father, which was not a good thing. His father was strict, and not in a good way. He always suspected his father of hitting his mother, but had never witnessed it and she'd never said anything. He had planned to apologize to Anna when he returned and agree to counseling.

Three days later she had still not returned. He'd called her mother on the second day to ask if she'd talked with Anna lately. He tried to make it sound casual but he was sure Ruth was suspicious.

On day three he was starting to panic and had intended to go to the police when Honey called. She was still working at the transit company because the corporation that had purchased them decided she would be hard to replace, given her years of experience. She told him she'd had a baby girl in July and she suspected it was his. At first she wasn't going to tell him, she said, but it turned out she needed financial help.

"How do you know it's mine?" asked Max with shock.

She explained that after their sexual encounter in the office back about a year ago, she became pregnant. She hadn't told him she'd gone off the pill because her doctor advised it. "I know you used a condom," she said, "but it must've been ripped or maybe you pulled out too soon. I wasn't gonna have an abortion, Max, and give up the only chance I might have of having a child. I know it's a lot to take in and I don't expect you to pay anything unless she really is yours, so we should do a paternity test. I'm sorry, Max."

Max didn't know what to say. He took a long moment and waited for his head to stop spinning before he said, "Don't be sorry, Honey. Why don't you come over so we can talk about it. And bring my daughter so I can see her."

Honey started crying, but then asked, "You want me to come to your house? How will that work? What will your wife say?"

"Right now, I'm not even sure I have a wife," he told her.

Honey arrived an hour later with her daughter, Michelle. Max started crying when he saw them. He told her the entire story of Anna taking his kids and leaving, and why.

Honey suddenly became concerned about her own welfare. "Max, I need to tell you that I've become a Christian and plan to raise my daughter as a Christian. When I found out I was pregnant, I went to a church and met the most amazing group of women, who took me in and took care of me. I never told you that growing up I was abused by my stepfather. I think that's why I was so promiscuous. I've been through a lot in the last few months and have had to make some pretty tough decisions, but the two most important things in my life are that I am now a mother and that I've given my life to Christ. I hope that doesn't turn you off."

"Just the opposite, Honey. I think you're the bravest woman I know. I think my wife left me because I abused her. When I lost my job, I started drinking very heavily and just had no life left in me. I had no education, no skills and felt worthless and I took it all out on her. I had been unfaithful to her during our marriage and I am ashamed of it and the way I treated her. The last time I saw her, she told me she would leave me if I did not change. Something inside of me snapped and I slapped her and walked out and went and stayed with another woman for a few days. I did get a job. I had applied as a long distance truck driver with Walmart and my license came through while I was away from her. When I went home no one was there except our cat and I haven't seen any of them since. I think she has left me and taken the children but I don't know where she would have gone. Her mother claims she has not heard from her but she might just be trying to hide them.

"Why don't you go to the police?" Honey asked. "They might be

in trouble."

"What if she just left me because I hit her? The police would have a million questions and I could lose the job I just started. I won't get another job like this one with a police record."

Honey nodded sympathetically. Max agreed to help her financially or said they could go to an attorney if she wanted to do that. Honey said she appreciated it very much. "Maybe you could just start by kicking in for the babysitter?" she asked.

Max assured her he would do as much as he was able. And no, he didn't need a paternity test. "One look at her and I know she's mine," he smiled.

A few days later, Max went to the local bar to see some of the guys. He had five days before his next run and was just hoping Anna would return before then. He was not going to mention his marital situation but his friend, Roy, said he thought he'd seen Caroline outside a building downtown, but when she saw him, she ran in the opposite direction. He was working for the water department and couldn't go looking for her.

"Don't you think that's strange?" he asked Max. "Why was she alone? I mean, I suppose it may not have been her, but it sure looked like her."

Max knitted his brow so Roy knew there was a problem. He nudged him and asked if there was anything wrong. Max asked if he had some time to talk.

"Sure, let's take a walk," said Roy.

Max told him everything, from the time he'd started being abusive to Anna and ending with his shameful sexual encounter with another woman that he'd just found out had resulted in a child. "And now Anna and the kids are missing. I'm afraid she left me."

"Holy cow, Max, that's quite a story," said Roy. "I had no idea you were going through that. I thought you were crazy about Anna. I'm sure she knows you wouldn't hurt your kids and she'll get her senses back and come home soon. Did you check with her mother?"

"Yeah, I called her mother but Anna wasn't there. She didn't ask why I was calling, though, which seemed odd. I haven't heard back from her, so I'm assuming Anna has contacted her by now with her whereabouts. I just don't know what to do," he said miserably. Then he looked at Roy. "Can you pinpoint when you think you saw Caroline?"

"Sure, I think it was on a Thursday, either the third or fourth Thursday in October."

Max knew he'd been out of town at the time, about halfway through his run. "Okay, thanks man. Hey, I'd appreciate it if you could keep all this confidential. I dunno how this'll turn out and you know how people talk."

"Sure, bud. Call me anytime you wanna talk, okay?"

Chapter - 54

Max went to Honey's later that afternoon and told her what Roy had said. She agreed with Max that it might be worthwhile staking out the site where Roy said he thought he'd seen Caroline. Max nodded and picked up his beautiful daughter and played with her while Honey prepared her bottle.

The next morning, Max went to the corner where Roy had been. He sat in his car and watched as people used a card to open the front door of the building Roy had described. He never saw anyone come out. He waited two hours. The next day he went at three o'clock in the afternoon. Again, he watched the front door but never saw anyone come in or leave. He was exhausted and went home.

The next day was Thursday, the same day Roy had thought he'd seen Caroline, so Max thought it might be a lucky day. He arrived around noon and finally found a parking spot, then left his car and walked around the building and sat on a bench across the street. Around one o'clock, he decided to get a cup of coffee at a nearby coffee shop. He noticed an attractive young woman with long brown hair in front of him in line. He sat and drank his coffee and when he was through, he noticed the young woman had purchased a to-go coffee bun and was walking out the door in front of him. She turned left and headed for the corner, but then Max saw a white van turn the corner and stop beside her. The driver jumped out and startled her as he opened the passenger door. Max almost walked over to see if there was a problem but then the young woman voluntarily got into the passenger seat and the driver closed the door. Max assumed it was a misunderstanding or lover's quarrel and walked back to the park to wait and see if he saw anything happening at the building. After another hour he returned to his car and went home.

Max knew he needed to talk with his mother. It was a conversation he was reluctant to have but he knew she deserved to know her grandchildren had been taken away. He had to own up to everything he'd done to Anna.

Honey and baby Michelle had stayed over last night so they could discuss Max's current predicament. He got up early on Saturday and said he had to leave on his next trip. Michelle had spent the night in Joey's crib in the bedroom across from them. Max felt a little guilty about it, since it had only been a couple of weeks since Anna had left, but he and Honey had made love the night before. He couldn't remember ever making love so passionately with Anna; he could not get enough of being with Honey. He knew he was falling in love more and more with Honey and if Anna does return there will be a problem. Right now it does not look like that is going to happen.

He left at seven the next morning, leaving Honey in bed and brought a sleepy Michelle to lie next to her mother. He kissed them both on the forehead before he tiptoed out of the house.

Chapter - 55

Approximately six weeks later

The phone rang at eight in the morning. Max happened to be home. He had just taken care of Moe and noticed he was not eating much. Could he be missing Anna and the kids or was he getting older? Probably the latter, he thought. It was Anna's voice on the phone. He initially was beside himself and started yelling at her but when she ignored him and he realized she had the upper hand he calmed down. "What is going on, Anna?"

"If you will just listen, I will explain everything to you. If you recall, you slapped me and left the house in a rant. I had no way to reach you and I frankly was at the end of my rope with you, Max. I want a divorce. I did not know what to do, so I sought out a shelter.

"A shelter? Roy, my friend, told me he thought he saw Caroline and I went there for a few days and just waited outside to see if I would see anything. I could not continue because I had to do my job. Why didn't you go to your mothers? I called her and she said she had not heard from you. Now, I know at least SHE was telling the truth.

"I did not want to go to my mothers, Max. I was ashamed that we were having problems, I was embarrassed for the children, I probably used bad judgement. But I did not know where to turn. I waited five days to see if you would come back and then I called my friend, Barbara, and asked her to look in on Moe until she saw your car back. I'm assuming he is alright."

"Where are you? I want to see my children," said Max with urgency in his voice. "I am sorry, Anna, for the physical hurt and the mental anguish I caused you. Can I do anything to help you and will you let me see my children?"

"While we were in the shelter the most incredible thing happened to us," said Anna.

"What, please tell me."

"We were helped by a volunteer that happened to start working there just a week or so before we came. She fell in love with our children. She realized the dire straits I was in and wanted to get us to a place of safety. You have to remember, Max, I was frightened of you at that time and had so much responsibility at once. I was worried about what this separation from you would do to the girls. I cannot tell you her name because it would break the rules, but she offered us $3,000 that she was going to buy a used car with and she helped find us a place to live."

"You have a place to live, Anna, and so do my children." Max started thinking of the situation with Honey and Michelle. He was not quite ready to break that to Anna, at least until he knew where they were.

"I am sorry, Max, but I can no longer live with you. It is hard to say, but I have fallen out of love with you. I never wanted to be married to a man that drank heavily and especially was physically abusive. You held it back for a long time, I have to admit, but I saw little chinks along the way of our relationship, but I ignored it, thinking it was my imagination. It wasn't."

"I know, Anna, but please know that I do love you and I love my children more than anything." He started crying and Anna could hear his sobbing. It was like the sobbing she did every night at the shelter.

"I will let the children know I spoke with you and you are missing them. I will call you in a few days with a date you can see the children. Is that okay?"

"Can you drop them off here?" asked Max. "This is their home."

"We'll see. They are in a great place and my landlord and neighbor is helping with everything she can. She adores the children. I did call my mother as soon as I got in this new home. She is going to come over next month to see us. I have found a great job very close to where we are living." She decided to leave it at that because she did not want to give him too much information at once.

"But you were going to be a stay at home mom."

"Not anymore."

Chapter - 56

Anna called Max approximately two weeks later and told him she was willing to bring the children over for a visit on the upcoming weekend. She had worked it out through her attorney a temporary visitation schedule until all the legal paperwork was started to garner her a divorce.

Max had admitted everything to her when they last talked about finding out he has a daughter by another woman. "I am not ashamed of her, Anna, how could I be. She is part of me and I can look at her and see it. Yes it was an affair, I admit that I was unfaithful during our marriage and I am terribly sorry for that. I wouldn't blame you if you never spoke with me again. But, Anna, you know how much I love our children. I would give my life for them.

"Honey has become a Christian. She had a very hard life growing up. No stable family life and she was molested by a step father at a young age. I find that to be disgusting. I would kill someone if they did that to one of my daughter's or son. Please consider this an admission of a terrible deed but what God created out of it is a beautiful little girl and I love her with all my heart.
I am truly sorry I hurt you, Anna."

Anna told him she forgives him and she is glad Honey had the baby. "I am sure she is a little doll. The girls will be so excited to know they have a baby sister." And that was all Anna had to say on the subject.

The children were dropped off on Friday evening by Anna and she met Honey and saw baby Michelle. She observed how much Joey and Michelle looked alike and smiled.

Anna went back to her car to leave. The arrangement was that she dropped off on Friday and Max would bring home on Sunday, but if his schedule does not allow, Honey will bring the children home. Anna could tell by talking to Honey that she was conscientious person and she trusted her children with her.

When the children came home on Sunday, they were very chatty and talked about eating pizza on Friday night and watching a movie with their dad. Of course Joey and Michelle were in bed early being that they were not even a year old yet. Thankfully, Honey was able to buy a crib at a yard sale for Joey and they had the bumper pad and sheets for a little boy even though it was in a girl's room. The decision was made that the children would stay at Honey's house on the weekends they visited because it was easier having all of the baby equipment there. Her house was smaller than the one Anna and Max had but it had a pull out sofa in the living room that the girls could sleep on. Things will change over the course of years.

Part - 5

Chapter - 57

Max and Honey had just gotten back from Washington, where their daughter, Michelle, lived with her family. After graduating with honors from UGA, she went to law school there and studied corporate law with emphasis on international. She landed a great job in DC, where she met her husband and now has two children. He is so proud of her. Honey is going to retire next month after 40 years at the transit system. He cannot believe she worked there that long, but it is sure helping their financial situation. He retired two years ago at 64 years old. He managed to save in his 401k and bumped it up to 22% the last five years he worked. Honey told him to do that and he was glad she did.

Fortunately, for them, Michelle got a scholarship for her undergrad. She had a 3.7 average in high school and was in the top 5%. She had to take out student loans for law school but he and Honey have been paying them for her. It was that or they wouldn't have any grands. They adore their two grandsons. Luke and Adam are seventeen and fifteen now, so they will be headed to college any day. Both are star athletes and with any luck maybe they can get scholarships. Their parents being attorneys are doing well. Luke Sr., we call him now is a criminal attorney and stays very busy.

Anna texted him this morning to remind him of the telecast tonight,

Real Mysteries, that she and Carolyn and Monica will be on. It has to do with the nursing student that disappeared back in 1991 when he and Anna were having their marital troubles. He doesn't like to think about that time because it really depresses him. At least things are better between them now. Anna agreed to shared custody when they divorced, so he was able to see the children on a regular basis and she allowed him additional visitation. He loved to take Joey to ballgames and he and Honey liked to take the girls along with Michelle, shopping for school clothes and other things. Honey made every effort to make friends with Anna, but it was awkward. Anna never warmed up to her, so Honey backed off after a while. All in all, their relationship was congenial and as gracious as possible. When Anna's mother passed both he and Honey attended the funeral and the same when Mrs. Eleanor Lee passed. Anna did the same when Max's mom finally passed away. She lingered in a nursing home for quite a while with dementia. He and Honey went as much as they could to visit her. He was glad he had his two sisters nearby that looked in on her often. It was a blessing when she did finally pass on.

They settled down on the sofa with popcorn as they usually did on Friday nights, if they did not go out. This was their special time together and it had become a ritual. The show started at nine o'clock. The previews ran during a commercial and made it look very dramatic. Once the show started Max finally got interested. The first scene was a school picture of Kathryn Morgan otherwise known as Katie, the narrator said. Max studied the picture and it gnawed at him that he had seen this girl before. They continued to watch as the story unfolded. He saw Monica and Anna walk up to the gate of their house, presumably for effect. The next scene was all of them sitting around. The others were introduced as the story kept unfolding. Apparently, the student went missing just after Anna and the children had moved out of the shelter.

The shelter, that is what he is remembering. "Honey, do you remember when I went to that shelter place for almost a week every morning hoping to see one of the children or Anna?"

"Yes, of course."

"Well, the last day I was there, I went into the coffee shop nearby after waiting in the park for over an hour and there was a girl in there that looked almost identical to the picture they showed at the beginning of the telecast.”

“Okay, so there is a possibility you saw her before she went over to the shelter that morning?”

“Not only that. I think I may have seen her being abducted!”

Chapter - 58

Max told Honey when he left the coffee shop he was behind her to pay his bill which was quick since he did not take anything with him. He was right behind her as she left and when he stepped out the door he watched her turn left to go toward the light, presumably to get the signal to cross the street. At the same time a white van turned the corner and stopped right beside her. The man jumped out and ran around the back and confronted her rather brusquely. He opened the passenger door and she proceeded to get it. I almost went up to them to see what was going on but she seemed so compliant to get in the van, I just thought it was a lover's spat or something like that. But, I am telling you, the girl looked so much like the one they just showed. After thirty years I can still remember her face. She was very pretty and young.

Honey listened intently because she remembered when Katie disappeared; it was all over the news and there were posters out everywhere around the campus, at least. "You have got to call Anna and tell her. Maybe she will know what to do. Max readily agreed.

He pulled out his cell phone and called Anna while the show was still on and told her his suspicions.

"Really? Oh, Max, we have to go to the police immediately. I am sure at the end of the show there will be a number, let's wait and see. If not, I will contact someone tomorrow and we will go and you can tell them what you saw, okay?"

Max said, "That sounds good, yes, let's do that. I will talk to you later then."

After the show ended, there was a phone number to the Syracuse Cold Case unit. Anna wrote it down and decided she'd wait until in the morning to call, then make plans with Max. She called Max's cell and let him know she will call tomorrow and asked his availability. "Anytime", he told her, "This,is too important."

The next morning, Anna called the number given on the broadcast. A detective by the name of Scott Jankowski answered and said they had received quite a few calls after the show last night. He asked how he might help her. Anna explained that her ex-husband had a possible encounter about the time Katie went missing and wanted to come in and talk with someone. The detective sounded skeptical, "I don't mean any disrespect, but how credible do you think this could be?"

Anna said, "He believes she was forced into a white van." At this information, the detective asked if they could come in today? Anna told him of course, and they set up an appointment for eleven o'clock. Anna called and told Max. He said he will pick her up so they can go in together. She agreed.

Max and Anna were greeted at the police department by Detective Jankowski. He asked if they would like any coffee, tea or water. They declined. He took them way down a hallway and into a room set up to be audio and video. But the Detective did not turn on anything.

Detective Jankowski started by saying, "This case is very old and until the TV producer for Real Mysteries came it had not been reviewed for a while. There are so many current cases, as you may well imagine, that we can only review cold cases when we have time. We technically have a cold case unit but it consists of only two detectives and I am one of them. So with all of that out of the way, tell me what you saw or think you saw."

Max explained that he had been in the area of where the shelter was for reasons he would rather not get into unless it was necessary. The detective nodded in acceptance and for him to continue.

"I had been sitting in a park for about an hour when I got up and walked down to a coffee shop. When I arrived there was a young girl sitting at a table drinking her coffee. I did not pay much attention to her but noticed her long brown hair and blue eyes. She was very pretty and petite. I sat down and drank my coffee but had other things on my mind and he looked over at Anna for a second. When I got up to leave she had gotten up herself and was in front of me. I remember she purchased a cinnamon roll and had them bag it up for later. Since I just had the coffee to pay for the transaction went quickly so I was on her heels as we left. I held the door open and she went to the left toward the light. I looked that way because I was parked across the street and could have gone to either corner to cross. I noticed as she approached the corner a white van turned the corner and a young looking man jumped out and ran around the back and approached her, opened the door and she got in. It appeared that they had words but she got in so quickly, I just thought it was a lover's spat and did not think any more about it. I went to the right toward the other light and the van drove past me through the green light. I don't remember anything about the van other than it was white and I don't remember what she was wearing. I am sorry, I don't have any other information."

The detective said, "Mr. Strickland, I do believe you may have witnessed the kidnapping of Katie Morgan."

He proceeded to tell them that there was a serial killer caught in 1993. At the time Katie was kidnapped there were two other women missing but it was outside of Syracuse. In 1993, there was a tip and a raid on a farm west of Syracuse. The farm was owned by Billy Moses and they found the corpses of four women on the property. He had three freezers in a barn where he had run electrical cords from a pole on his farm. It was very haphazard. The freezers were empty. But there was evidence that there could have been bodies in them. We had a cadaver dog verify it. We had no DNA however so there was no one to link to. If he got rid of the frozen bodies there is no telling where he put them. Katie's remains washing up on the beach in NC is a possibility that he took the bodies to the seashore and rented a boat to take them out in the ocean to dump them or he just dumped them over a bridge. I hope others will eventually turn up. By the way, Mr. Moses owned a white van.

"What happened to Billy Moses?" asked Max.

"He died in prison. Killed by another prisoner, happens all the time."

Chapter - 59

Anna called Marie Morgan as soon as she got home. She told her Detective Jankowski would be contacting her as well but she wanted to hear it from her first. "Of course, they don't know for sure if Katie made that fate, however the chances are probably that she did since Max saw her get in a white van and this Mr. Moses had a white van. I am not sure why the police did not connect the dots back when Katie went missing but they apparently didn't."

Marie said, "I am glad you called Anna, really I am; it is just such a shock. Larry is not here right now. He is out doing his favorite pastime, golfing, but he will be as shocked when he finds out. I guess we just wait for the detective to call and see how he wants to handle it all. Thank you for calling. And please tell Max we are so glad he remembered it. I guess the TV show being done did trigger a lead after all."

After they hung up, Marie called Ally and told her everything she knew. Ally was so pleased to hear there finally are some answers. "It is so troubling though that someone can just be snatched off the street!"

Marie said, "I agree. I think he must have had a knife or a gun and threatened Katie. She would not have had but a split second to do something. I hate to think of what he did to my baby before he killed her. I just hope and pray she did not suffer for too long."

"I know, Marie," as Ally started choking up. "Let's just remember

Katie as the beautiful soul she was and know she is in heaven waiting for you and Larry. She was a lucky girl to have such terrific parents."

Marie was sobbing and could hardly talk so Ally just told her she will check on her in a few days and hung up.

Ally called Neal and filled him in on everything. "I will be coming down in a few days, Ally, so we will have our good cry then, okay sweetheart?"

Ally said, "Okay, I love you." They hung up knowing they were growing close and every time they were together, they did not want to leave each other.

Epilogue

Ally knew Mary was at home so she just walked up there carrying a bottle of chardonnay. When Mary opened the door, she could tell from Mary's expression that something had happened. They had grown so close as friends, they could almost finish each other's sentences.

Ally started telling Mary the horrible story of Max realizing he probably witnessed the abduction but at the time had no idea that was what it was. He was out of town for two weeks driving his load for Walmart and did not hear the news about Katie. By the time he returned it was barely in the news. Remember, he and Anna were estranged, in fact he did not know where she was so of course, he was distraught. All these years later when he watched the Real Mysteries episode and saw Katie's picture it started coming back. He and Anna, his ex-wife went to the police together and reported all of this and that is when they found out there was a serial killer at that time Katie went missing but the police never connected it because of where they were finding the bodies of the first two women. It was way west of Syracuse. He was arrested sometime in 1993 and sent to prison and was killed in prison.

Mary was spellbound by all of this information. "And just think, it all began with you, Ally."

"What do you mean?"

"You contacted the local police and found Katie's parents and from there you worked hard at getting information. You really cracked this case. Real Mysteries did their part of course but your sleuthing did help, admit it. Actually, didn't I mention to you that my husband's aunt went missing in Atlanta Ga before he was even born and the case has not been solved to this day. What do you say…want to work on it?

Ally shook her head, "No, I want us to work on it together. Now, please go and pour us a glass of wine!"

Acknowledgements

This book was very much a collaborative effort starting with the first readers of the manuscript: my husband, Larry and my dear friend, Barbara Weakley. Barbara went on to be my first editor, just as a favor. She spent countless hours reading and re-reading and I am in her debt. Colleen Lewis, is another dear friend that read the first manuscript. I trusted her judgement and honesty and knew she would tell me to throw it out if she did not like it. Thankfully, she did not tell me to throw it out. Instead, she told me it was a good story which encouraged me to continue. I also want to acknowledge Teri M. Brown, author of two recent award winning books. When I met her at a local book signing, she did not hesitate to tell me to call her and we ultimately met for breakfast and she has continued to be a source of support and information. My editor, Lisa Messinger, was a delight to work with and her great advice will help me in my future endeavors. She was kind enough to slog through the first manuscript of this new author and I am profoundly grateful. **Jinal Peterson did a beautiful job with the cover.**

I also want to thank my husband, Larry, for his support and love. During the final hours of getting this book ready, we were forced to put our oldest Maltese, Gabby, down. In his grief he supported my efforts in making a deadline that I had promised my formatter, Jinal. Lexi is our third and final Maltese and is a sweet fur baby. I extend thanks to all of my friends that supported my efforts and helped me through this sad time. Another special thank you to Lisa, my editor, who, herself a pet lover and encouraged me through these last days.
Lastly, I have had a medical condition that is mentioned on my website. It is called Burning Mouth Syndrome and there is no cure. Strictly controlled by medicines and lozenges and lots of water. I also want to thank the Facebook BMS groups that I am in for their support.
They of course do not know I am writing a novel, but their words and prayers are

precious to me. I love and pray for them, also. One day, hopefully, a cure will be found.

Sincerely,
E. L. Boyer

www.boyersbookshelf.com
Facebook: e.l.boyer_author
Instagram: e.l.boyer_author

About the Author

E. L. Boyer is a retired RN. She grew up in Atlanta, Ga. After living in Ohio for ten years, she and her husband, Larry, moved to coastal NC and she retired a few years later. She loves to golf, play Mah Jongg, but mostly read. She adores her little Maltese named Lexi.

She is currently writing her second book, in which she continues with the Ally Malcom character, whom she made up out of thin air but now, she cannot get out of her life. She hopes the reader will want to find out what Ally is up to next.

You can reach her at liz@elboyer.com as well as her website www.boyersbookshelf.com